SARA, NICHOLAS
—AND THE—
LAST DRAGON

KATHLEEN MURPHY MCILROY

 FriesenPress

One Printers Way
Altona, MB R0G 0B0
Canada

www.friesenpress.com

ISBN
978-1-03-913339-6 (Hardcover)
978-1-03-913338-9 (Paperback)
978-1-03-913340-2 (eBook)

1. JUVENILE FICTION, LEGENDS, MYTHS, FABLES

Distributed to the trade by The Ingram Book Company

Dedicated to my darling daughters, Tara-Lea and Lindsay-Ann

TABLE OF CONTENTS

CHAPTER 1

THE KING'S REQUEST

"I don't care what Mom says, I'm bored and I am going outside! So what if I have a fever," mumbled Sara.

She was determined to spend some time outdoors after being cooped up in the house for three long days with a nasty flu-like bug. Longing for some fresh air, Sara wanted to spend time in her backyard—her very own magical place that she could escape to, surrounded by a high privacy fence with a swing that her father had hung for her from one of the branches of their large maple tree. All along the inside of the fence was a beautiful rose garden her mother had planted, with every type of rose you could imagine. There were white, yellow, pink, red, and even lavender and apricot-coloured roses. Their heavenly scent wafted throughout the yard.

A shy girl, with no brothers or sisters, Sara had frizzy blonde shoulder-length hair and pretty blue eyes, but she had to wear glasses to see better. Already feeling very self-conscious around the other kids, she had recently gotten braces. Just the thought of

1

facing her schoolmates gave her a knot in her stomach because they treated her monstrously. Last year at school, a group of girls had bullied her endlessly. Every time she was in the halls they laughed at her and amongst the whispers and giggles, she overheard them say that she was an "ugly geek." They called her a "four-eyed nerd." These hurtful words made Sara very sad and lonely, causing her to prefer sitting by herself in her bedroom or under the shade tree in her yard reading a good book instead of venturing out into the neighbourhood to play. Adventure stories and fantasies about kings and princesses from days of old filled her mind. She daydreamed about meeting and falling in love with her own knight in shining armour one day. You could say she was a loner and a dreamer. It was the last week of summer vacation, which had been a welcome break from school. While most kids were going to the mall or the movies, getting together with their friends, swimming, and playing sports, Sara stayed home. She definitely didn't want to go back to school.

Her mother had gone to run some errands and grocery shop, leaving strict instructions for Sara to stay in bed. But she wasn't expected to be back until sometime after lunch, so out to the back-yard Sara went, with a blanket to sit on and a snack to nibble on. The sky was blue, spotted with a few white cotton candy clouds. She shook her hair back as a gentle breeze caressed her face. It felt so good compared to the stuffy house. Reaching for some cheese and a cracker, she listened to the songbirds. Noticing a ladybug land on a leaf beside her, she scooped it up into her hand and made a wish, saying, "I wish I was pretty and not so shy, so the other kids would like me." Then she blew the ladybug off her hand and it flew away, disappearing over the fence.

Still feeling a little weak, she decided to lie back on her blanket. Adjusting the hood of her housecoat that was bunched up under her upper back, Sara stretched out her lily white legs to get some sun on them. The buzzing of a bumble bee caught her attention as she watched a ruby-throated hummingbird drink from the feeder and abruptly flit away. Closing her eyes, a smile crossed her face as she inhaled deeply, smelling the sweet fragrance of the roses. They smelled so much better than the store-bought kind. Sara pushed the nose piece of her glasses up as she always did and felt a tickle on her leg, only to discover an ant heading up her nighty, so she quickly flicked it off. Overhead, the fluffy clouds floated by, transforming from one shape to another. One resembled a horse running, with its long mane and tail flowing behind, while another looked like a dog with floppy ears, in a sitting position. She yawned.

Then out of the blue, Sara was startled by a large mechanical crane rising up above her fence line, way up, higher and higher, past the roof tops. Curiously, she watched as it finally came to a halt and a man in the bucket contraption on the end began to work on the power lines. Sara imagined a dangerous dragon clutching a man in its mouth.

Off in the distance, she heard a woman's voice calling, "Nicholas! Nicholas!"

I'll bet that's his mother, she thought. Of course she meant the new boy who had moved into the house next door. Sara had seen him last week when she swung very high on her swing and could see over the fence into the neighbouring yards. Up until then, she had never been very interested in boys, but this new one was especially dreamy, Sara thought, and he looked to be just about her age. Ever since she saw him, she couldn't stop thinking about him. "I wonder if he'll be going to my school and if he might even be in my class," she pondered, smiling. "Maybe we could study together and walk to school together. He might even carry my bookbag for me." But she was far too timid to ever approach him and introduce herself or ask how old he was or what grade he was going into. She always felt awkward around other kids.

As the clouds continued to drift by, Sara yawned again and she noticed one that looked very much like a sailboat, its sail stretching until it was long and skinny and deformed. Feeling quite drowsy, she decided to rest her eyes for a bit and the next thing she knew there was a most magnificent cloud. It looked exactly like a castle with turrets and appeared to be built of white marble that glistened in the sunlight and sat high atop a hill overlooking a vast kingdom.

The base of the hill was surrounded by a moat of water with a great stone wall around it. A wooden drawbridge stretched across the moat from the hill to an iron gate in the wall where people entered. The kingdom was made up of several shires, the castle being in Ivanshire, in a fertile region where most of the families were farmers. A wide river meandered through Ivanshire and on to the next shire.

Although there had been peace for many years, there was a time when terrifying giant dragons had walked this land, burning villages, destroying forests, and killing people. Some of them were winged dragons that flew and some were fire breathing. But thanks to courageous knights, they had been hunted and conquered. All except for one, that is, the last one, the granddaddy of them all, Old Bellow. He had been put to sleep by magic many years earlier.

"Nicholas! Nicholas!" a voice called. "The king has sent me to get you because an unimaginable thing has happened. Word has come that the last dragon, Old Bellow, has awakened and is terrorizing the kingdom. He has already burned two villages to the ground in the southern shire. Their villagers are fleeing to the highlands in the north. There is no telling how long it may be before he makes his way here. You must come at once. You are our only hope. The king's own men are all too cowardly and refuse to go after Old Bellow, but his grace believes you may be different. He has seen you in the tournaments, challenging the fiercest opponents. You were brave enough to challenge the Black Knight three years ago. It has been said that you are fearless and faithful to King William, that you are a man of courage. Please come to speak with his grace."

Nicholas, a handsome, muscular young man with shoulder-length, wavy fair hair and light blue eyes, was well tanned from working in the fields every day, ploughing, sowing, and harvesting. Confident, but not overly, Nicholas never shied away from a challenge. Upon hearing such alarming news, Nicholas set down the harness he had been holding. He couldn't believe his ears and shuddered to think of actually seeing a real live dragon, let alone coming face to face with one. They were the stuff of nightmares, of the legends passed down from his father and his grandfather. He was reminded of the story his grandfather had told him about the dragon Faz. He told the king's messenger, "When my grandfather was a young boy, a dragon flew over the countryside spewing fire on the forests, burning them to the ground. Everyone had to run away to the next shire to escape its wrath. My grandfather and his family hid in a field of tall corn, so afraid that they would be spotted if the fire-breathing dragon, Faz, flew overhead. But after two days of hiding, without eating, in the cold and darkness at night and no sign of the dragon, they thought it was safe to come out of the cornfield, only to have the beast approach them swiftly overhead. My grandfather told me that he was so scared that he closed his eyes while his mother held him close. He could hear the flapping of the wings and feel the breeze from Faz flying so near to them, but somehow his family was unseen by the dragon and they were spared. In a few days they heard rumour that a knight had speared Faz to death, so the folks from their village were able to return to their homes—the ones that hadn't been torched, that is. My grandfather's was one of the lucky families that had a home to go back to. Most of the village was smouldering and had to be rebuilt. As Grampa grew up, so did the trees in the forest once again."

Having no family to answer to and knowing he might be able to help, Nicholas didn't hesitate to agree, "Lead on then, sir. There is not a moment to lose." He was very brave, although some perceived his bravery as recklessness. His philosophy was, what will be, will be, and he believed his fate was out of his hands. "Old Bellow has been asleep at the bottom of the river since Sir Nigel defeated him with the magic the Wizard of Windsor gave him. How could this be? What evil force could have awakened that beast?" he wondered aloud.

It being very early in the morning, Nicholas had been up feeding his livestock. Taking a quick look around the barn to make sure there was nothing else of importance to do before leaving, he hurried to the stable to mount his horse. His flock of sheep baaed and bleated.

Knowing the urgency of the situation, he quickly followed the king's messenger past several stone cottages with thatched roofs, smoke plumes rising from their chimneys in the cool morning air, through the town square where the farmers' market was just coming to life for the day, and along a cobblestone road. The butcher was preparing to open his shop as well as the tannery and the cheese factory. They were all unaware of the possible danger heading their way. Nodding at a friend as he passed by the mill at the water's edge, the young man and the king's messenger finally came to the gate at the stone wall that surrounded the moat. The messenger gave the signal to have the gate raised and the drawbridge lowered and they crossed over and continued along a dusty road that led up the hill to the castle. Extremely nervous to be meeting the king, Nicholas was astounded by the sight of the spectacular white castle. Several of the king's courtiers were milling about and watched as he entered the courtyard. When they reached the royal stables, their horses were taken from them and Nicholas was ushered into the castle, which felt very chilly with its white marble walls. Their footsteps echoed as they continued through a great hall to the throne room, where King William awaited.

King William was known to be the most kind of all the monarchs in many years and was beloved by most. He was very generous, and would give grants of land and lend money to villagers when asked for help, as long as they repaid him when they could. The king arranged for entertainment for his subjects by holding tournaments in the great arena, that were open to all who wished to take part.

Nicholas was one of the many who enjoyed the mock battles and competitions. As a young boy of seven, he began training to be a knight, as page to a lord. Then he became a knight's squire or apprentice at fourteen. His job was to look after his master's armour, dress him for battle in the arena, and serve him food. If a squire is able to pass all the tests, he is dubbed a knight at about the age of twenty-one. But Nicholas's parents had died tragically and he was left alone to care for himself and their farm, unable to continue his training. He often entered the jousting competitions using all he had learned, and in time, he became a champion. His reputation was that of being fast and steady with a strength that usually left his opponents sprawled on the ground.

With eyes widened, he gazed around the large throne room. Nicholas was awe-stricken. He had never been in such a wondrous structure in his life. This grand room felt warm and cozy in contrast to the hall. The ceiling was high and vaulted with curved oak ribs for support. The walls were covered in decorative oak panels with beautiful sconces shedding candlelight into the room. Enormous iron candlelit chandeliers hung from the ceiling. On one wall there was a roaring fire in a very large stone fireplace flanked with tall cabinets with bevelled glass doors, their shelves filled with books. The sunlight flooding in through pointed, arched stained glass windows shone onto magnificent colourful tapestries that hung on the walls.

On the opposite side of the room there was a very large oval table surrounded by several chairs, upholstered with purple velvet, where Nicholas imagined the king and his knights would sit and talk. The legs of the table and chairs were intricately carved. Pewter and silver platters, goblets, and such filled the shelves of more cabinets. Beautifully painted works of art panels hung on the walls, while ivory and stone sculptures of earlier kings were set around the room.

Bowing to the sovereign, Nicholas thought to himself, *What splendour!* King William sat at the end of the room upon one of two ornately carved high-back thrones. He wore a blue, belted full-length silk tunic over tights and a purple velvet robe lined with white ermine fur and his gold crown. The mood of the day was reflected in his aging face.

In a worried tone, he said, "It is with a heavy heart that I have summoned you here, lad. I assume my messenger has told you of the dire situation?"

"Yes, Your Highness. It is unimaginable!" replied Nicholas, his shoulders tense.

The king continued: "Let me just say that I have admired you in the arena for a few years and have great faith in your ability to help us now in this time of peril. Everyone else has refused my request due to family obligations. I do not know how on earth this beast has awakened. It was magic that stopped him before. It must be a very strong and evil force that has brought this monster, Old Bellow, out of its deep sleep. Legend says that the Wizard of Windsor has the strongest good power in the land. I greatly fear whatever or whoever it is that has defeated that power now. If you do not try to do something, we may all perish. If I were a younger man in better health, I would pursue Old Bellow myself, but I am afraid I must entrust it to you. You shall be provided with whatever you may need for the journey: horses, food, water, weapons, blankets, and gold coins. Whatever you want. Old Bellow was last reported in the village of Aaron, which is not long from here. Please tell me you will at least try to save our kingdom. I am ashamed of my royal guardsmen and knights for their cowardice. We are depending on you, Nicholas. I beg of you, give me your answer."

CHAPTER 2

PRINCESS SARA

A t that moment, there was a loud creak as a heavy wooden door opened and a young woman entered the throne room. Nicholas turned his head to look and saw her, dressed in a purple gown brocaded with gold that was closely fitted across her upper body while the skirt billowed outward. Her cloak was blue velvet, lined with white ermine fur. She wore her silky golden hair braided and looped on either side of her head and a gold bejewelled crown sat on top. Her face was rather plain but her eyes were the brightest blue Nicholas had ever seen, like sapphires.

"Oh, I beg your pardon, Uncie, I thought that you were alone," she said in a gentle voice. She glanced over at Nicholas and coyly looked away. Nicholas was spellbound by her presence. Suddenly, the tension fell away and a new sensation came over him. He was overcome with tingles throughout his body.

"That is quite all right, my dear," answered King William. "Come in. Allow me to introduce you to my gallant guest. I have requested his aid to save us from the deadly dragon, Old Bellow.

He is about to give me his answer. Perhaps you could help me persuade him. Nicholas, this is my dear late sister's daughter, Princess Sara. Sara, meet Nicholas of the family O'Hara." There was a long silence as Nicholas and Princess Sara's eyes met and they both seemed bewitched.

Then Nicholas cleared his throat. "Ahem," and bowed with respect as the princess offered her hand to him and he took it and gently kissed it, saying, "It is truly an honour to meet you, Your Royal Highness."

Sara was the only living relative of King William and of course led a very privileged life. She had everything she could want—except for friends. Her parents had died of influenza during an outbreak in the kingdom a few years earlier. She and the king had a very close relationship. Extremely independent and headstrong, Sara never hesitated to speak her mind or let her feelings be known to anyone, including the king. She said in a forthright manner, "I recognize you from the games in the arena. I enjoy watching them with my uncle. I greatly admire your courage." Thinking him very handsome, she added, "It is a pleasure to finally meet you."

Breaking his gaze, Nicholas said, "You need not say anymore of the task, Your Grace. I shall try my very best to find and slay this last dragon for you. But I will need those provisions. I have a long journey ahead to the land of Windsor, where I must seek the wisdom of the wizard. Only he can advise me as to how to conquer such a beast as Old Bellow." As he spoke to her uncle, Princess Sara studied Nicholas's face and mannerisms.

Impressed with him, the princess said, "Oh, Nicholas, the land of Windsor is so far away through the forbidden Black Forest and beyond the Crystal Mountains, with who knows what dangers lurking. You are so courageous. Promise me you will take great care. We would be eternally grateful if you could stop this terrifying threat to the kingdom." Then, turning to the king she blurted out, "Uncie, I have an idea. Let me go with Nicholas. He should not have to face this grave danger alone. I can help him. You know I am well trained with a sword. Please let me go."

To which he responded, "That is out of the question my dear child. I am sorry but I cannot possibly allow you to go."

Disappointment obvious in her expression, the princess said, "Well, then, Nicholas, my prayers will be with you and I truly hope to see you when you return."

"Thank you, My Lady. I shall do all I can," said Nicholas. Looking into his eyes once more and smiling sweetly, Princess Sara walked up to him and kissed his cheek. He savoured the enchanting scent of her perfumed skin. She was so very graceful and had an air of self-confidence about her that appealed to him.

"Fare thee well, Nicholas. I shall await your return," she said.

"Farewell, Your Highness, until we meet again," said Nicholas, his eyes following her every step as she turned and left the room. He felt butterflies flitting around in his stomach.

"We are forever in your debt, Nicholas. Let us go and get you geared up for your journey. I will introduce you to my soldiers and then you can select a horse of your liking," the king said, rising from his seat.

"That will be fine, Your Grace," Nicholas responded, following alongside. They walked to the soldiers' quarters, where Nicholas was introduced to the men and then escorted to the stables. As he strolled past the stalls, he saw there were many beautiful chargers from which to choose.

Stopping alongside one, he joked, "This large, tan-coloured horse with the blonde mane seems to want me to choose him. He keeps nudging me with his snout. How old is this steed? He is exquisite and looks strong and agile enough for a lengthy journey."

The stableman replied, "He is three years old, sir."

"That seems perfect. I will take him then. What is he called?" asked Nicholas.

"His name is Liberty, sir, because he was so hard to tame. He put up a good fight for his freedom before we broke him in," the stableman explained. Liberty stood seventeen hands high.

Stroking the horse, Nicholas said, "Hello there, Liberty, my friend." Liberty snorted and whinnied. "You will make a fine companion. You are a handsome devil. I hope you are up for a long ride." Carefully packing his saddlebags with such supplies as food, lambskin bags of water, blankets, furs, changes of clothes, knives, and bow and arrows, he noticed a gleaming sword and took it, as well.

Arrangements had to be made for the care of his farm during his absence. Nicholas had taken care of his family farm ever since his parents, Warren and Grace O'Hara, had also died during the flu epidemic that had ravaged the kingdom. So he was kept busy raising the sheep and working the fields himself. He had no other relatives. The young farmer was hard working and well liked by everyone. Never having a bad word to say about anyone, he enjoyed a good laugh with his friends once in a while. And then whenever there was a jousting match he would enter, even though they were generally reserved for knights. Nicholas had earned himself a reputation and was encouraged to participate in the king's competitions.

After receiving a lance and gleaming shield, Nicholas chose a suit of armour, which was a shirt of chain mail, made from linked rings of iron, and a shiny metal helmet to wear when the time came to face Old Bellow. He fastened them to his saddle and proceeded to mount the charger.

The time had come for him to say his farewells and depart on his dangerous quest. The king said, "Thank you, Nicholas, and may luck be with you. We shall all pray for your success and safe return." He held out a beautiful engraved silver sheath and, from it, drew a sword. "I want you to have this sword. It was my father's and his father's before him. Since I do not have a male heir, I think it would be appropriate if you took it. Perhaps it will bring you good luck."

Moved by the gesture, Nicholas accepted the sword, saying, "Thank you, Your Grace. I am truly honoured to have been chosen and I shall do my utmost." He slipped the silver sword in his belt and handed back the one he had previously chosen and King William led him out to the courtyard where all his men lined the road that led down the hill to the drawbridge.

The soldiers cheered him on, yelling out, "Hail, Nicholas, hip, hip, hurrah!" They admired him for undertaking such a terrifying task. As Nicholas left through the gate, he looked back at the castle and up to a tower where Princess Sara was waving to him. She blew him a kiss. That kiss would spur him on his way to face the unknown danger that lay ahead.

A tear trickled down Princess Sara's cheek as she watched the valiant yet humble champion ride down the road and over a ridge and disappear from sight. Although they had just met, she had strong feelings for him. She spent most of her time with her uncle or ladies in waiting, and was lonely. With both parents gone and no siblings, the princess longed to meet someone to marry and eventually have a family of her own. She couldn't help but wonder if Nicholas would ever return from such a horrible mission and if he didn't, how terribly sad she would be. What would become of their kingdom?

CHAPTER 3

INTO THE UNKNOWN

It was a bright, sunshiny day to begin his journey. Nicholas's emotions were all over the place. On the one hand, he was beaming with joy after meeting Princess Sara, but on the other, he was filled with uncertainty, knowing that he was undertaking such a perilous quest.

He said to Liberty, "Well, my friend, we are on our way. You do not know it, but we are probably heading into grave danger, possibly death. Nevertheless, I feel it is my duty as a loyal subject to try my best to save the kingdom. I find it hard to believe that no one else came forward to help. I think the princess liked me, do you not, Liberty?"

He and his equine companion cantered through the village and galloped on along a bumpy dirt road through the countryside, a gentle breeze brushing his face. They rode by pastures of cattle and sheep and fields of wheat, barley, potatoes, and corn, past other villages, heading toward the grassy plains. There were woods of oak and maple, pine and cedar trees alongside the road they travelled, a sprinkling of colourful pretty wildflowers, and a beautiful scent in the air that reminded Nicholas of Princess Sara. The winding road met up with a river. Every so often Nicholas spotted birds flying and squirrels scurrying up and down the trees. At one point he nearly trampled a fox that dared run across the roadway directly in front of him.

Hour after hour he rode on with no one to talk to, finding himself thinking of his mother and father and wondering what they would think of him taking on this dangerous mission. He imagined their excitement after learning of his meeting the king and princess. After a while, Nicholas noticed his surroundings and said aloud, "Hmm, there are fewer and fewer trees. I think we are nearing the plains, Liberty." When they did arrive at the plains, Nicholas said, "It is so flat, it appears to go on forever." It was just lush, green grass as far as the eye could see; the river still ran alongside the road. They cantered across the plains for a couple of hours and Nicholas was amazed to suddenly see a large herd of wild horses congregated by the river ahead, drinking. Some were in the water. There were probably fifty of them, all different in colour and markings, and when they caught sight of Nicholas approaching, they scattered in all directions.

"Such majestic creatures," he said to himself. Thoughts of Princess Sara were foremost in Nicholas's mind. "What an enchanting lady she is," he said to Liberty. "Ahh, I can still smell her beautiful perfume. I wonder if, when I come home to the village after slaying the dragon, the princess will greet me with a kiss and an embrace." His stomach was doing flip flops as he entertained the idea. "Maybe, just maybe, she would marry me if I asked her."

Humming a favourite melody, he trotted along, the landscape turning into scruffy brush. But he suddenly stopped dead in his tracks, saying, "Liberty, look there, a person standing in the middle of the road ahead!" To his surprise, when they got closer, the dark figure just seemed to melt into a black puddle on the ground.

"What? How very peculiar," said Nicholas with a puzzled look on his face. At that moment, a chilling gust of wind blew past him and a chorus of cawing rang out from a group of very large crows that were perched on the bare branches of a single dead tree at the side of the road. Their eyes seemed to follow him as he passed by, making Nicholas feel very uneasy.

He squeezed his eyes shut then reopened them, saying, "I think my eyes are playing tricks on me. How about we find a place to rest for a while, my friend? You must be as tired and thirsty as I am." He led Liberty to the river to drink and roll in the sand on the riverbank to cool down. Looking around, he drank from one of his waterskins. He lifted the leather cover of his saddlebag and took out a primitive-looking map and said aloud, "I need to chart our journey to the land of Windsor. Far ahead beyond the badlands in the distance, I think I see the faint tree line of the Black Forest. The king has declared it forbidden to all of his subjects. Legend says that evil lives there. We will need all of our courage and wits to survive it."

Feeling confident that he knew which direction to take, Nicholas leaned over the river and refilled his waterskin before tying it to his belt and cantering off again. They clipped along at a brisk pace, the river eventually winding away from the road and out of sight and the green grass getting browner and sparser. Nicholas and Liberty only had each other and there was a special bond forming between them. Reflecting on the events of earlier in the day, the news of the dragon, Old Bellow, meeting the king and princess, Nicholas didn't think it felt real at all. It was a day he wouldn't soon forget. "I cannot wait to see her again, she is so wonderful!" he said to himself, fantasizing.

Still pondering how things might unfold upon his return home, Nicholas was suddenly jerked forward by Liberty who neighed wildly and his legs seemed to buckle beneath him. The steed began to sink into the ground.

"LIBERTYYY!" gasped Nicholas. Looking around them, he realized that they had ventured into quicksand. "Do not move, Liberty. That will only make it worse. Let me try to get you out." At once, he slipped out of the saddle and was horrified as he, too, began sinking into the sand. His arms flailing, he yelled frantically, "Help, someone, HEEELP!" Then reaching out for the edge where the ground was solid, he grasped hold of a root or something but it broke off due to his weight. The frightened animal snorted and neighed in a frenzy and struggled in vain to escape the pit. Nicholas clasped hold of one of Liberty's saddle straps as they both began to sink farther down.

Below the surface of the sand was a bed of thick mud, and each time he made an effort to get out, Nicholas got sucked down a little more. After struggling repeatedly and sinking deeper and deeper, he felt there was no way out of this crisis, with no one anywhere in sight to help. A terrible hopeless feeling washed over him as he listened to his charger's desperate cries. His eyes welled up with tears and, in his panic, he thought, "Oh, Lord, I will never see home again or Princess Sara. I have let her down and will never have a life with her as I imagined." In a sorrowful tone, he said, "Liberty, I am so sorry, old friend. I have failed you. Alas, I have failed everyone in the kingdom."

By this time his horse was up to its withers in the sand and muck and Nicholas was up to his neck. He made one last desperate effort to escape the hold of the quicksand to no avail and then, as if from out of nowhere, an enormous snow-white eagle appeared above them. It had a massive wingspan of probably two metres from tip to tip, the likes of which Nicholas had never seen. Shrieking and swooping down around them, fluttering its huge wings rapidly, it seemed to suggest that it would help them. As the eagle hovered overhead, Nicholas reached up and grabbed hold of one of its large talons. Then he clutched Liberty's saddle strap with his other hand

and yanked with all his might while the bird flapped wildly, rising upward with every ounce of strength it had.

The young man and his horse started to rise out of the quicksand but he lost his grip of the strap because of the slippery mud and Liberty plunged back down into the pit, gushing mud into the air like a geyser. The giant eagle continued to flutter over them. Once again, Nicholas grabbed hold of his panting steed and the eagle thrust upward, shrieking loudly and flapping its enormous wings. It was a horrendous struggle but finally the bird miraculously pulled them completely up and clear of the mud and sand and gently lowered them onto a solid area of ground.

Gasping rapidly for air, Nicholas lay on the ground beside Liberty until he eventually caught his breath and calmed down. He had never been so scared in all his life. Feeling relieved and grateful, he turned to the great white eagle, but it had vanished. In an effort to calm his horse, he said, "There, there, it is all right now, my friend. We are safe. Easy now." The young man stroked Liberty's muzzle and petted him until the animal stopped trembling. Then he stood up and reached into the mud-laden saddlebag, pulled out a rolled-up blanket and attempted to wipe as much of the mud off the animal and himself as he could.

With Liberty settled down, Nicholas said, "I had better check to see if all my gear and food are intact." Examining the contents of his saddlebags, he said, "Excellent, everything seems to be here, except my lance is missing. It must have fallen into the mud and been sucked under. That is most unfortunate because I had specifically imagined piercing the dragon with it." His helmet and sword and shield were still attached to his saddle but were caked with mud, along with pretty much everything else. Spending at least a half hour, Nicholas cleaned everything off to the best of his ability.

With the sun now sitting lower in the sky, he felt this would be a good time to bed down for the night. "I will gather some kindling and start a fire to roast one of the rabbits that I brought.

Here, Liberty, you have some oats." After preparing and eating his meal and removing Liberty's saddle and blanket, the weary farmer lay down by the glowing fire on his bedroll, listening to it crackle. His eyes lit up when he noticed wide ribbons of light dancing in the night sky. Overhead, breathtaking streaks of green and blue, pink and purple rippled and waved to his delight. It was the aurora borealis. He was mesmerized by the dazzling show for a while, but was so exhausted, he couldn't keep his eyes open and so drifted off to sleep.

CHAPTER 4

UNEXPECTED VISITOR

I t was early afternoon when Nicholas was startled awake only to see Liberty's head hanging directly in his face, snorting and nudging him, as if to say, "Let us be on our way." The first thought that popped into his head was that of Old Bellow and the dreadful situation at hand. "You are absolutely right, Liberty, Old Bellow must be stopped, and we are the only ones to do it. Let us eat and make haste," he said, brushing his hair out of his face with his fingers. With that, the heroic farmer got up to rekindle the fire with a stick, roasted a fowl to satisfy his hunger, and began to pack up and secure his gear. He was just about to start on his way when he heard the sound of hooves approaching. "Oh, now who could this be?" he said to Liberty.

Turning his head to look, Nicholas saw a dark grey horse and rider and when they arrived at the camp, he couldn't believe his eyes. It was none other than Princess Sara. What a surprise. No longer wearing an elegant gown, she sported a pair of brown breeches, a blue tunic top, and riding boots. Her silky golden locks were tied back in a ponytail and she appeared to have full saddle-bags and a helmet and sword fixed to her saddle.

"Your Highness, what are you doing here?" asked Nicholas, raising his eyebrows in curiosity. "This is no place for a lady." The butterflies returned to his stomach.

"Nicholas, I could not let you go alone and since none of the knights volunteered to accompany you, it is not fair and I am quite capable of helping you find the wizard and Old Bellow. I promise I will not be a hindrance. I have been trained my entire life in the art of fencing," she replied confidently.

Nicholas was flabbergasted. "His grace could not have permitted you to come? He will be furious when he finds you have made this choice. You must go back."

"No! I am not leaving. Now please, I will not discuss it further. Let us proceed," she said.

Sensing a stubborn streak in the princess, Nicholas figured there was nothing he could do or say to change her mind. So, he now had the responsibility of guarding the life of a princess as well as slaying a dragon. "Very well, then, let us be on our way, but I beg of you, please stay close," he implored with a sigh. And they set off in the direction of the forbidden forest. He couldn't get over the fact that Princess Sara had come to join him. He was overjoyed at the thought, yet worried for her well-being.

At first they ambled along, side by side, talking for a while. They told each other about themselves, discovering that they had both lost loved ones to the horrible flu epidemic, which left them both lonely in life. The fragrance of her perfume drifted through the air beside Nicholas, a reminder of her blowing a kiss to him. The farmer turned hero told the princess about his horrible brush with death in the sinking sand and how he was saved by a mysterious enormous white eagle. With eyes like saucers, she listened to the terrifying details. Her heart sank when she heard that he had almost perished. In her mind, Sara was hoping to share a future with him.

Nicholas said, "How is it that you were able to leave the village unnoticed? I would have thought his grace would keep a closer eye on you."

"I just slipped out for a predawn ride, which I often do. I love that time of day when the dew is on the ground and no one is awake but the birds. I suppose, by now, Uncie may be quite worried about me, but he refused to let me join you and I could not stay behind and just wait for your return. I tried to obey him but all manner of horrible thoughts was going through my mind." Sara reached for his hand and held it, squeezing.

Nicholas smiled at her, saying, "I am glad you came. I did not want to leave you either and wondered if I would ever see you again." They both felt great fondness for one another. "We should pick up the pace, I think. Follow me." He took the lead and they rode at a controlled gallop. Sara kept her eyes on the back of him as the wind blew his hair and she thought about how strong and handsome he was. She felt safe in his company. Noticing the landscape beginning to change once again, Nicholas realized that they were entering the badlands region. There was a very dry heat and the ground beneath them had become hard and cracked. He wiped the salty sweat that was stinging his eyes from his brow, as he listened to the hooves pattering on the narrow path that had replaced the road. Hearing a single loud caw, he spotted a huge raven sitting on a crag from the corner of his eye. He felt a sudden chilling gust of wind. Turning his head to look at the raven, it seemed to be staring directly at them as they passed by and Nicholas was horrified to see that it was holding an eyeball in its beak, giving him goosebumps. He sped past the gruesome sight without pointing it out to the princess for fear of alarming her.

As time went by, the sun beat down upon them, casting long, skinny shadows over the ground. Their gallop slowed to a trot as the blistering heat zapped their energy and that of their horses. Nicholas removed his cloak and rolled up his tunic sleeves; his throat parched, he could feel the sun burning his face.

"We must stop for a drink, Your Highness, it is so hot. Are you well?" said Nicholas.

"I am fairly weary and very thirsty and you need not address me in that manner any longer. Sara will be fine by me," she said. They stopped for a rest and quenched their thirst. Sara wet a handkerchief from her waterskin and dabbed her face and neck to cool herself after rolling up her sleeves. She had never felt so hot and tired, but didn't want to let on. She couldn't let Nicholas think she was weak and unable to actually help with the mission they were facing.

As he gave the horses some water, Nicholas asked, "Who taught you how to use a sword?"

Sara replied, "I was instructed by one of the knights, Sir Kenneth. He was the best. He was a close friend of my father but got very ill and died a few years ago. I miss my mother and father and Sir Kenneth. Why did everyone I love have to get sick and die? All I have left is my uncle now."

Nicholas, understanding the feeling, just looked down. To help the princess feel better, he said, "I do not know why it is that bad things sometimes happen to good people. But these sad events in our lives just make us stronger, I think. They build character." Then remembering the task at hand, they resumed their journey. There was absolutely no vegetation for many kilometres. This place was barren and uninhabitable.

"What a horrid place this is," the princess said, hoping it would soon cool down and become more pleasant.

"Yes, I definitely agree," said Nicholas, unable to stop thinking of impending danger and worrying for Sara's safety as well as his own.

CHAPTER 5

THE FORBIDDEN FOREST

I t wasn't long before they arrived at the edge of the feared Black Forest. "So here we are at the forbidden Black Forest! Well, let us get through it. We can do this, My Lady," declared Nicholas, looking around. Thinking of all the frightening legends he'd heard about the Black Forest, he felt the sudden urge to flee, but gave his head a shake and took a deep breath.

With a scowl, Princess Sara said, "Nicholas, I told you to call me Sara, do you not recall?" She, too, was remembering the horrible tales she had been told as a child about this place, but felt so safe with Nicholas.

"Oh, yes, I am sorry, it is a force of habit. I shall try to remember, Sara," he replied. Two very large, old, crooked trees with gnarled branches and enormous bowed trunks seemed to mark the entrance to the woods. Apprehensively, Nicholas took the reins of the princess's horse and guided it through. Upon entering, the tree branches magically entwined, closing off the entrance. There was a strange loud, rubbing, creaking sound as all of the old trees surrounding the forest tightly butted up against each other and thick vines intertwined with the tree branches, connecting one to another, forming a wall. It was as if they were being imprisoned. Princess Sara gasped. Swallowing, Nicholas stood motionless. It was as dark as a cauldron and they couldn't see anything around them. He wondered what they had gotten themselves into. There was a nasty odour in the air, like dead animals combined with mould. The wind eerily whispered through the trees.

Sara's voice quivered, "Nicholas, are you there? I cannot see you. I smell evil in this place."

"I am right here beside you, My Lady, I mean, Sara. Do not be afraid. Here, I will take your hand." He had Liberty walk directly beside the princess's horse and he reached for her hand. Sara felt the soothing warmth of his hand; knowing she was with Nicholas relieved any anxiety.

"I will be fine now. You lead on and Storm and I will follow right behind you," she said.

"You must stay very close, do you understand?" Nicholas said as he began to gingerly trot along an overgrown path through the woods. It was very dim and dank.

Chilling hoots and howls of unseen birds and animals could be heard. His pulse increasing, Nicholas shivered, barely able to see the trail. He depended on Liberty's instincts to keep to the path. Sara's horse, Storm, followed directly behind Liberty. Unable to see much, they kept on, dodging branches and dangling vines along the way, all the while hoping to reach the opposite side of the forest as soon as possible. Nicholas inhaled sharply as a tangle of vines caught on his cloak like someone was tugging on it. Thinking he heard rustling and footsteps behind him, he whipped his head back to look, but couldn't see anyone. Just the outline of trees. But the young man couldn't shrug off the feeling that they weren't alone and every so often he turned to check behind him. He wanted to ask the princess if she had seen anything, but decided not to for fear of upsetting her, so he just smiled at her. Gradually, their eyes adjusted to the darkness of the forest and they could see the outlines of things but no details.

Unexpectedly, a large vine slapped Nicholas in the face. "OW!" he gasped. But it was no vine, it was a snake! It dropped onto his shoulder and slithered around his neck. Then he felt a sharp sting. "OUCH!" he yelped.

"Nicholas, what is it? Are you hurt? He had been bitten. Grasping hold of the snake, Nicholas hurled it away from him into a tree trunk with a thud and flung his sword back and forth in case there were any more snakes hanging in their way.

"It was a snake and it bit me on the neck. Clasping his neck with one hand, he moaned, "Ohhh, that hurts! I just hope it is not poisonous."

"Oh, you poor dear, let me see." Sara drew close enough to him to see his neck. "It looks very red and sore around the punctures. Do you want to stop?"

Grimacing, Nicholas shook his head and continued on more cautiously, listening for anything approaching or stirring. But the bite area on his neck became extremely swollen and inflamed. Agitated by this unfortunate occurrence, he muttered, "It is probably infected." Feeling woozy, Nicholas groaned feebly to Sara, "Ohhhh, my head is spinning, I do not feel well at all."

"Please stop, Nicholas. Let me try to get the venom out," Sara said. She pulled up alongside Liberty and sucked the puncture wound on the stubborn hero's neck and spit it onto the ground. She did it a second time. "There. Hopefully, that will prevent you from getting sick. You should feel better soon." Light-headed and disoriented, Nicholas slumped forward on his horse. Liberty carried on.

"Oh, Nicholas!" Princess Sara said. She realized that there was nothing she could do except continue to follow behind Liberty and hope that Nicholas would get better sooner rather than later.

With her one hand clutching the handle of her sword and the other holding the reins, she watched all around her, ahead and behind, but could not make out much in the dimness of the forest. At one point she thought she saw the dark figure of a person ahead, but as they drew closer, it vanished from her sight so she just assumed she was mistaken.

After a while, Nicholas, feeling less dizzy, sat up again. "I am feeling better now. Do not worry, Sara."

"Oh, I was not. I trusted you had stamina." she chuckled. Trotting slowly through the hanging vines and foliage, it occurred to the young man that he hadn't seen any wildlife scurrying about on the forest floor or through the tree branches and it had become extremely quiet.

"Do you not think it odd that we have seen no birds or animals of any kind since we entered these woods?" he asked. Then, a cold wind rushed by him and he thought he saw the dark shadow of a person standing ahead, but in the blink of an eye, it was gone. "My mind is playing tricks on me, Sara." And then as he looked down at the ground, he noticed that it appeared to be moving.

"What is . . . what on earth? SNAKES! AAAAH! Hundreds of snakes all over the ground!" he blurted out in horror. They were writhing and slithering all over each other. "Liberty, hyah!" Nicholas commanded, squeezing his heels hard into the ribcage of his horse. "We have to get away from these serpents! Hurry, Sara, hurry!" With Sara following directly behind him, Liberty galloped and Nicholas swung his sword to and fro, hacking through the vines and foliage until finally the forest floor was still. They were clear of the snakes—just earth, moss, and leaves were underfoot. Panting frantically, the duo stopped to calm themselves. Sara was a little shaken by the thought of so many snakes.

"Ohh, how ghastly!" she exclaimed, drawing her shoulders up in disgust. Nicholas's snake bite was still hurting so Sara gathered some moist earth and put a poultice on his neck. "Here, this should ease the pain and draw out any more poison," she said.

His throat very dry, Nicholas asked, "Sara would you like a drink of water?" He reached for a waterskin attached to his belt, only to discover that it was gone. "That is strange. It must have loosened and fallen along the way. We will drink from the other one in my saddlebag." It was still there and they shared the water with the horses, who had worked up a lather, as well. Remounting, he said, "We had better press on if we are to get out of these woods before nightfall."

"Yes, absolutely!" Sara nodded in agreement. Suddenly, Liberty neighed loudly and bucked, almost throwing Nicholas off. A multitude of bats poured out of a dead tree trunk beside the path and flew directly at them, dipping and swooping around their heads. There were hundreds of them. Their piercing shrieks in unison and the deafening sound of all their wings flapping were overwhelming.

"AAAAAH!" they both screamed. Their first inclination was to duck, throw the hood of their cloaks over their heads, and swiftly gallop away. With Storm hot on the heels of Liberty, the bats trailed behind them.

With one plight after another happening, Sara yelled in frustration, "We are getting out of these woods if it is the last thing we do!"

"Do not worry, Sara. Everything will be all right. I will not let anything bad happen to you," Nicholas assured her. And then, as if something else suddenly caught their attention, the cloud of bats abruptly changed direction and flew off, en masse, leaving them alone. "Phew! Thank goodness. How very unusual. There is something very off here. Something is not right." Pointing, he said, "Look, a clearing over there. We should rest. I will get us something to eat." After getting to the clearing, Nicholas dismounted and reached for his food supply from one of the saddlebags and found it to be missing, as well. "Oh, no! What mischief is this? I will have to hunt something for us to eat, Sara." But then he discovered that his bow and arrows were gone. "Now this is getting serious. Oh, wait, surprisingly, my sword is still here." Grabbing it, he climbed up a tree and sat on a branch, hoping to see a bird or animal to spear.

As she dismounted, the princess said, "Luck be with you and please hurry back." She petted Storm while giving him a drink of water and watched in vain for birds and waited for Nicholas to return. She, too, felt that something was amiss in these woods.

Nicholas sat in the tree, waiting and watching. There was a disturbing stillness. All that could be heard were distant snapping branches and the rustling of the wind. No animals or birds could be seen anywhere in the forest. After waiting long enough to convince himself that there would be no meat for supper, he climbed back down. Returning to Sara, he said, "How curious. For some unexplained reason there are no birds or animals in this forest."

"I spotted several blackberry bushes a short way back. Maybe they will do," said Sara. So they ventured back to them on foot.

Lifting the bottom of their tunics to form pouches to carry the berries, they picked several handfuls each of the plump, juicy fruit. And what a very welcome tasty treat it was, which they shared with their equine friends, enough to stifle their hunger for the time being.

More eager than ever to get out of the forbidden forest before nightfall, the pair set off once more. Passing a leafless tree, Nicholas noticed another enormous raven sitting on one of its branches. Again it cawed loudly and seemed to stare right at them and he felt a current of cold air brush past him.

"Well, it seems there is one bird here after all. Oh, Lord, it is holding the stub of a finger in its beak!"

"Oh my goodness, what?" Sara shuddered. Now she sensed someone was nearby watching them but she couldn't see anyone.

Nicholas decided he should keep one hand on his sword just in case they encountered danger. Reaching behind, he couldn't feel it on his belt, causing him to stop and dismount apprehensively to search for it, but the sword was gone.

"Oh, no, Sara! Now my sword is gone! This is not good at all. What is happening?" he said, irritated, with a scowl on his face. "What are we to do now? What has happened to all of these things?"

"How could anyone or anything have removed your gear without my noticing," said Sara. "I have only glanced away from you and Liberty briefly this entire time. I do not understand." Then peering down at Storm, she exclaimed, "Oh dear, my entire saddlebag is gone now, as well." Climbing back on Liberty once more, Nicholas steered them toward the dim glimmer of light that shone through the trees on what appeared to be the outer edge of the forest.

"I cannot wait for us to get out of these woods," he said severely. At that moment, a vague buzzing sound could be heard from up ahead. Buzzzzzzzzzzz. . . . It grew louder and louder. Buzzzzzzzzz. . . . It sounded like a swarm of bees. "Now what on earth!?" said Nicholas. Then they saw it: a huge black cloud moving down to the ground ahead of them. It hovered there.

"What is that? asked Sara. And then it hit them like a brick wall: a horrible putrid smell, the pungent smell of death. As they approached the large black mound, the buzzing sound became deafening. BUZZZZZZZZZZ. . . . "Oh, Lord, that smells!" Sara said, holding her handkerchief over her mouth and nose to avoid inhaling the foul odour. BUZZZZZZZZZ. . . .

Looking at the mound, they saw it appeared to be moving. It was! It was an enormous swarm of flies on top of the carcass of some large animal that must have been dead for quite some time judging by the sickening smell of it. Beneath the cloud of flies, maggots covered the dead animal. In fact, as they watched, Nicholas thought it looked more like a few carcasses, judging from the number of bones he could see. His eyes surveyed the area only to discover a pile of skulls off to the side of the path. They looked to be human skulls!

"Ugh! Come, Sara, quickly!" he gagged. "Hyah, Liberty, hyah!"

Barely able to keep from retching, he galloped away like a flash of lightning with Sara following right behind him. She, too, had seen the pile of skulls. There were many scary sounds. Terrifying sounds they'd never heard before.

"What creatures are making these sounds and where are they? I never see any animals!" Sara cried out in earnest. "Who were those dead people? What happened to them?"

Once again, Nicholas thought he saw the shadow of a person disappear behind a tree. Feeling rattled and sharply jabbing his heels into Liberty, he yelled, "Hyah, Liberty, faster, we are not spending one night in this godforsaken forest with unknown creatures lurking about! Sara, keep up!"

Sara, noticing the path ahead had widened, dug her heels into Storm to dash forward faster, and overtook Nicholas. She sped ahead of him, grinning because she sensed that he thought she was just a weakling and she knew otherwise. Her strength would show itself on this quest. Galloping rapidly toward the light, Sara and Nicholas swung their swords back and forth in front of them to ward off anything in their way. The buzzing grew fainter and fainter until they could no longer hear it. All of a sudden, there was a loud thud to the left of them. Liberty was startled and bucked up, throwing Nicholas to the ground. His head hit a rock, knocking him unconscious.

Sara screamed, "Nicholas!" and jumped off her horse and ran to his side.

CHAPTER 6

THE MOLE CREATURES

A short, stocky, furry brown creature with a long tuft of hair on the top of its head waddled over to them on its hind legs. Another one jumped down from a tree and joined it. They grabbed Princess Sara. She kicked and screamed and they were joined by two others that proceeded to paw over their belongings, grunting to each other.

The princess yelled, "Unhand me immediately. Let me go! I must tend to Nicholas, he is hurt." But one of the creatures silenced her by gagging her with her own handkerchief. After a while, Nicholas came to. His head throbbed with pain as he lay face down on the ground and he opened his eyes. Rolling over, all he could see was a brown blur. It took him a minute to recollect what had happened. He remembered hearing a thud and flying off Liberty.

"Saara," he groaned. His vision started to clear and he saw that he was surrounded by several of these little furry creatures, the height of children, and that his wrists had been bound together with vines. Off to one side of the group he spotted Sara, sitting on the ground against a tree trunk, bound, as well, and gagged. "Sara!" he yelled.

Nicholas gasped at the sight of the unusual looking creatures. They walked upright like people but were entirely covered in fur. Their faces were very humanlike but hairy. Raising his hands to the cut on his head, he discovered that there was blood trickling down his forehead over his left eye. A few more creatures jumped down out of a tree and came up close to study him with their beady eyes and he recoiled. They began to poke and prod him with sticks and their hairy fingers, opening his mouth, feeling his teeth, and grunting to each other.

Struggling to break free, Nicholas cried, "Stop that! Who are you? Let us go. What have you done to Sara? Where are our horses?" They continued to grunt, seemingly understanding each other. Then some of them snarled and nudged the duo to their feet and pushed them along a path to a large hole in a huge tree trunk that led down under the forest floor. "Unhand us, you oafs! Where are you taking us? Let us go! Do not worry, Sara, I will get us out of here," he shouted, resisting.

Suddenly, the creatures growled violently with a wild look in their eyes, exposing long fangs. Sharp claws sprung out of their paws. Sara glared at Nicholas in horror and he decided to cooperate. They were shoved into the hole in the tree trunk and they tumbled down a few metres, landing with a thud on their behinds, blind in the darkness. They were in a long underground tunnel.

What they couldn't see was a series of additional tunnels branching off from this one, leading in different directions, with chambers off the tunnels and two more creatures standing there to meet them. One growled and pulled Nicholas to his feet and pushed him along and shoved him into one of the chambers. The other pulled Sara up and pushed her into another room.

Nicholas cried out, "Sara, be strong. I will find you and rescue you!" Trying to struggle free of the vines binding his wrists, he made a valiant effort to escape past the creature, but it growled fiercely and tackled him to the dirt floor. It was extremely strong and grunted and growled, convincing Nicholas that it was pointless to try to wrestle with the dangerous creature in the dark, so rather than be overpowered and likely killed, he decided to cooperate. It wasn't until he heard the creatures shuffle away that Nicholas realized he had been left alone in the chamber. He was scared, not being able to see and not knowing where he was or what was going to happen as well as being worried about Sara. His head throbbing, Nicholas felt helpless, knowing he had to find Sara and escape to save the kingdom from Old Bellow.

He called out, "Sara? Are you there? Are you all right, my lady?" There was an earthy smell and it was cool and damp in this den. Reaching out in the darkness to feel around, he stood up and stepped forward, immediately tripped over something, and fell to the floor. "Ouch, what was that?" he said. Getting back up, Nicholas hit his head on something hard and furry. "Arrgh," he yelled sternly. With his arms outstretched, he felt what seemed like a dry animal pelt dangling. Frustrated, he continued to slowly explore. Feeling the wall, he hugged it as he walked around the perimeter of the room. And then he stubbed his foot into something hard and flinched in pain. Next, he felt a soft pile and sat down on it. "This is safer for now," Nicholas said, annoyed.

Meanwhile, in Sara's chamber, she sat against the wall on the dirt floor, struggling to free herself of the gag in her mouth by holding up her bound wrists and grabbing hold of the handkerchief with her fingers. She pulled and tugged on it with all the strength she could muster. She bit at it and, after several tries, she succeeded and called out to Nicholas.

"Nicholas, are you there? Are you well? Where are you? I'm coming for you."

In time, her eyes got used to the darkness and she was able to see her surroundings. It was a crudely furnished room with a table made of logs and stumps for seats. The walls and low ceiling were dirt with roots dangling out. There were wooden bowls and numerous baskets, woven of vines, filled with berries, nuts, and mushrooms from the forest. Deciding to look for Nicholas, she stood up, brushed herself off, and cautiously snuck out of the room into the tunnel. She checked both left and right to see if any creatures were around and when she saw that the path was clear, headed along the underground tunnel.

Nicholas's eyes adjusted to the darkness as well and he saw that he was sitting on a bed of leaves. Standing up, he noticed a large wooden bowl on the floor. "Oh, that must be what I tripped over," he said. Dead birds and rabbits hung from the ceiling to cure. "So there were some animals, after all." A large keg of what appeared to be water stood in one corner of the room. "These creatures actually live, eat, and sleep underground like moles. They are mole people," he said to himself. Extremely thirsty, Nicholas badly wanted a drink from the keg but thought it could be tainted and make him sick. Determined to find Sara, he checked the tunnel to the left and the right for guards and when he saw that it was empty, he headed out of the room and made his way along the tunnel, watching for the creatures. Then he spotted Sara approaching and they ran to each other.

Sara said gleefully, "Oh, Nicholas, here you are and you are all right!. I was so worried about you. What are we going to do? We must get out of here," she implored. Above ground, a large group of the furry creatures was examining Liberty and Storm with great interest. One of them climbed up on Liberty's back while the others watched and Liberty started to buck and run wildly. Grabbing hold of his mane, the creature held on for dear life but eventually fell off. He grunted for joy. This was a wonderfully novel experience for him. Liberty trotted over to the entrance in the tree trunk where he had seen Nicholas and Princess Sara taken. The furry creatures gathered around him, forced him back to the clearing, and held him still while another one of them mounted him to get a ride. Liberty threw him off, but after multiple attempts by the creatures, he finally gave in. They took turns trying to ride him. Then another group of the creatures started to ride Storm, who cooperated from the start.

Out of the silence came a faint groaning and moaning sound from farther along the underground tunnel. It sounded like someone or something was in terrible agony.

Sara said, "Nicholas, do you hear that? Someone is hurt. We must help them." The couple made their way to the doorway of the chamber where the groans originated and entered the room, which was furnished much the same as the others, and, to their surprise, there, lying on the bed of leaves, moaning, was an old man. He was very pale and thin. His grey hair was very long and messy and he had a long, scruffy grey beard. The man was curled up, clutching his stomach, rolling from side to side. The expression on his aged face was one of anguish.

When he saw Nicholas and Sara, he sat up and yelled with delight, "Humans! Oh, my prayers have finally been answered. Have you come to take me home? The saints be praised."

Looking down at the old man, Nicholas answered glumly, "I am sorry, sir, but we have just been captured by these mole people ourselves. I don't know what they want with us. Who are you? How long have you been here? Could you please untie us?"

"Ohhhhh," the old man groaned, lying down again.

"Are you ill? What is it?" asked Sara.

"I do not know why, but I have been getting these horrible stomach cramps off and on," he replied with a pained expression on his face. Raising himself up again, he said, "My friends call me Zoz. I hail from the village of Duncan to the west of the Black Forest. I have been a prisoner here since the day I ventured into these forbidden woods three months ago. See, I have been keeping track of the days on the dirt walls here," he pointed. They could see that the walls were covered in groups of six lines with strokes through them, one for each day of the week. Zoz rose and began slowly pacing back and forth as he continued talking. "I know it was a foolish thing for me to do but I wanted to see the Crystal Mountains just once before I died. My whole life I have heard the legends of their magnificence and even though I was warned of the dangers of trying to get there, I had to see them for myself. I am not getting any younger, you know, and am alone in this world, so I figured I had to fulfill one last dream. I set out hiking and camping and the very day I entered the forest, I was jumped on from behind and captured by those miserable little furry creatures. They brought me here to this den. They have not killed me, even though I have often wished they would, but they will not let me go. I suspect they are trying to fatten me up in order to eat me. At first they seemed to be harmless enough, curious creatures, and I thought I was like a trophy to them, but they have very sharp teeth and claws and can snap suddenly and turn vicious if you do not behave. They keep bringing me food and insist that I eat. What is your story, lad? Why have you dared to enter the forbidden Black Forest, and with a lady, no less?" He grabbed a knife made of sharpened bone from the table and cut the vines that bound their wrists.

"Many thanks, Zoz," Nicholas said as he rubbed his wrists and then ripped part of his sleeve off to dab his headwound.

Sara took the cloth from him. "Here, let me take care of that for you," she said, and blotted his wound and then bandaged his forehead with her handkerchief. "Fortunately it is not a serious cut and the blood has already clotted, but we will put this on anyway."

"Thank you, Sara." Nicholas proceeded to tell Zoz of his quest to find and kill the last dragon, Old Bellow, and how he was on his way to the Wizard of Windsor for his assistance and how Princess Sara had run away to join him.

"What? A dragon! I thought there were no more dragons. The last one of those monsters was put to sleep for eternity, I thought," said Zoz, flabbergasted.

"Well, it seems he has awakened and is causing chaos. Did you see anyone else in the forest other than these mole people?" Nicholas queried. "We saw a pile of dead bodies and I was sure something else was lurking in there, watching us. Have you anything to drink? I am so thirsty."

"I did not see anyone else in the woods, but I, too, had a nagging feeling that I was being watched. Maybe it was the mole people. I have some tea made of roots that is quite good or some rainwater in this keg. Help yourself, lad, and you as well, Your Highness."

"Oh, thank you." Nicholas reached for a cup and ladled some of the beverage for Sara and then for himself and eagerly drank it.

Gulping the tea, Sara said, "Mmmm, this is so good. I needed that. May I have some more?"

"Of course, please do," answered the old man. "Ohhhh!" He doubled over in pain again. "Oooh, I really need to see a healer. If only they would let me leave." Sara ran to his side and stroked his back to ease his discomfort.

"Have you ever tried to escape?" asked Nicholas as he drank.

"Oh, yes, but every time, one of those creatures was waiting in the tunnel or at the exit. Maybe we could plan our escape together," said Zoz enthusiastically. Liking that idea, the trio decided that they would try to sneak out then, while the tunnel appeared unguarded. Little did they know that it was a very good idea since the creatures' attention had been diverted by the horses. Nicholas grabbed a mouthful of berries and they loaded up with as much of Zoz's food as they could carry. Leaving the chamber to look for waterskins or wineskins to hold some water, they ventured down the tunnel a short distance and saw the entrance to another room.

As they neared it, they discovered a vile odour permeating into the tunnel, and when they looked in, to their horror, they saw a decomposing body lying in a huge pool of dried blood and the walls appeared to be splashed with blood. Gasping, they lurched backward and quickly scrambled along the tunnel to another room on the opposite side.

"Ahhhhhhh," screamed Sara as she spied, hanging from the ceiling, two more rotting corpses that appeared to have been brutally attacked and partially eaten. "Oh my Lord!"

There was blood splattered all over the walls and floor. Nicholas, Sara, and Zoz ran swiftly down the tunnel toward the exit where the daylight streamed in. Noticing one more chamber near them, they peered in and, to their delight, found it just happened to have their bows and arrows and other belongings piled in a corner. They squealed with joy.

"So that is what happened to our supplies. Those little thieves! What savages!" said Nicholas as he collected his missing things and flung his saddlebags over his shoulders. Sara joined him and grabbed her belongings, as well, and, cautiously, they walked to the opening in the ceiling and climbed up the ladder made of roots. Poking their heads outside, they could barely open their eyes, after being in the dim underground space, especially Zoz.

"We will have to wait while our eyes adjust to the light again." Sara said. So they waited for a few minutes until they were able to see outside and saw that all of the mole creatures were several metres away in a large clearing, huddled around Liberty and Storm. They seemed so thrilled and involved taking turns riding the chargers and having so much fun with this new and exciting amusement that it would be easy for the three prisoners to slip past them and run to safety. When none of the creatures were looking in their direction, they made a run for it as fast as they possibly could, reaching a dense clump of trees out of the creatures' view. Stopping there behind the trees to catch their breath, they looked to see if they had eluded the mole creatures. Seeing that they had successfully escaped, they continued to run toward the setting sun at the edge of the woods. Zoz, because of his age and aching gut, had a hard time keeping up, but he ran like his life depended on it until he keeled over from pain and exhaustion.

"Nicholas, wait! Zoz has collapsed," Sara yelled. Looking back and seeing Zoz on the ground, Nicholas ran back to his aid and advised Sara to keep running.

"Come, Zoz, get up, man. Just a little farther and we will be out of this forest. You can do it. Lean on me. We are almost there," he said. Putting his arm around Zoz's waist while clutching his armour and supplies, they continued on together and met up with the princess at the outer wall of trees. There was no opening for them to escape through. Realizing they were trapped in the woods, Nicholas took out his sword and hacked away at a cluster of branches and vines between two tree trunks. The forest didn't want to let them go and immediately the vines entwined to close the opening back up. Nicholas desperately thrust his sword through, cutting over and over. Sara joined in with her sword until there was a space large enough and with Zoz helping to pull the vines apart, Nicholas aggressively shoved Sara through and then he and Zoz squeezed through. They all collapsed to the ground and lay there, panting.

Not long after, Zoz propped himself up on his elbow and said, "I am beginning to feel better. Perhaps it was the lack of fresh air and sunshine that made me ill. This is amazing, I feel so good for the first time in weeks." The tall, thin old man stood up and Nicholas noticed a healthier colour return to his face.

Although pleased about that, Nicholas said, "But what shall we do about our horses? We cannot leave them there with those mole creatures. I cannot possibly carry on without Liberty and Sara must have Storm back. I guess I shall risk a shrill whistle, hoping that Liberty will hear and make a run for it." So he did and a short while later they heard the faint sound of hooves galloping through the forest heading in their direction. As the sound of hooves grew louder and louder, Zoz pulled the vines to the side, while Nicholas and Sara rapidly cut a larger opening with their swords. The Black Forest kept tangling branches and vines together but the duo slashed and chopped harder and faster until they had cut away enough of the trunk for a horse to fit through. Liberty approached with Storm following. Now they, too, had escaped from the mole people. Zoz held the vines apart while Nicholas forcefully guided the stallions through the trees and out into the clearing.

"Ha ha ha. How wonderful!" smiled Nicholas. "Come, Zoz, you ride with me. Let us get as far away from this wretched forest as we can," he said and the three hastened away toward the Crystal Mountains.

CHAPTER 7

THE CRYSTAL MOUNTAINS

When the trio had travelled an hour or so, they neared the foothills of the Crystal Mountains. It was twilight and the sun was sinking into the horizon, painting the sky a beautiful deep orange, streaked with pink and mauve.

Looking up, Zoz said with a grin from ear to ear, "Look! Just look at that white mountain range glistening in the sun's rays. Is it not breathtaking, just as I knew it would be? Oh, happy day. I have finally realized my dream." He took a deep, long breath and exhaled.

Nicholas nodded in agreement. "You certainly were right about it being magnificent. I never imagined anything so spectacular. Sara, is it not beautiful?"

"Oh my, yes, how absolutely amazing. And to think I never would have seen this wonder if I had not come to be with you, Nicholas." They stood still for a moment just taking in the awesome view of the Crystal Mountains.

Nicholas said, "We will have to find a place to spend the night soon. Zoz, do you see the light reflecting on the mountainside up there?" He pointed. "That looks like the opening to a cave, does it not? That is just what we need. Let us keep going until we reach it and we will camp there."

"That sounds good, Nicholas. I cannot wait to get off this horse and eat something. My rear end is killing me and my stomach is growling."

Princess Sara said, "Yes, I am so tired. This has been the longest day."

It was dusk by the time they got to the cave. Zoz was so excited about actually reaching the mountains. "This is the happiest day of my life. I cannot wait for the light of day tomorrow when we will get a better look at the mountain's beauty. Make haste, Nicholas, let us take shelter and get a good night's sleep."

Nicholas lit a torch to help them see their way into the cave. Once inside, he saw that it was a small, empty cave with shiny white marble walls. "Oh, good, there is a flat area, large enough for the three of us to make a campfire and lay down to sleep and the horses can go over there," he said, pointing to the left side of the cave. "I will get Liberty and Storm settled, remove their saddles and tack, and give them some food and water. Sara, I am going to scout around for some kindling for a fire. I shall return shortly."

He handed the torch to Zoz and lit a second one for himself. After seeing to the horses, Nicholas got his and Sara's bedrolls and a couple of fur blankets from their saddlebags along with some game and berries from his food supply, put them in the cave and headed out to collect firewood. Shivering, he noticed that a full moon had replaced the sun and felt the night air was much cooler than during the afternoon. It was a clear, starry night and the moon illuminated his path. As he collected a bundle of twigs and branches for the fire, Nicholas was fortunate enough to witness another natural wonder—a meteor shower. He watched in amazement while several stars fell in the sky, leaving bright, glowing trails, and he returned to the cave excitedly, saying, "Come, look, the stars are falling. It is amazing!" Zoz and Sara ran to the cave opening and watched in wonderment as the stars showered down, one after another. Breaking away from the celestial show, Nicholas started a fire to take some of the damp chill off in the cave while Zoz and Sara continued to observe the phenomenon. Then the three of them sat by the flames, cooked and ate the meat and finished with berries, all the while swapping tales of their lives back home. Zoz told them that his wife, Kep, and his son, Tholl, had died from the plague a year earlier and how he felt compelled to make the journey to the Crystal Mountains. They were all exhausted after their full day of adventure, so they decided to retire and covered themselves with blankets.

"Good night to you, Zoz. See you in the morrow. Oh, and I forgot to thank you for being there today. Otherwise, we probably would never have escaped," said Nicholas, feeling his head wound, which was only a little tender. "Good night, Sara. I am glad you are with me. See you in the morrow."

"Likewise, lad. You saved my life! I am eternally grateful. Good night, Your Highness. It is an honour to have met you."

"Oh, please, call me Sara, Zoz, and good night to you both. Sleep well," said the princess and as she was dozing off, all she could think about was how exciting it was spending this time with Nicholas. With a deep sigh, Nicholas gazed up at the sky through the cave opening to watch for a few more shooting stars and, within minutes, he heard Zoz snoring. Not long after, he, too, fell asleep.

Morning broke and Nicholas was awakened by a stream of bright sunlight pouring into the cave. Wiping his eyes, he looked out of the cave opening, thinking of the challenge that lay ahead of him and knowing they would have to hustle and eat and start their journey. The mountain range was extremely beautiful as the white rock glittered and sparkled in the light of the sun. It was the combination of marble and quartz crystal that gave the mountains their gleaming white colour. How glad he was to be able to share the spectacular sight with Princess Sara, who had just opened her beautiful blue eyes and sweetly smiled at him. Nicholas smiled back. "Good morning, Your Highness. How lovely you look first thing in the morning. Did you sleep well?" Nicholas said with a grin.

"Thank you and good morning to you, Mister O'Hara. I do not think I have ever slept so soundly. Mind you, I do not think I have ever been quite as exhausted as I was last night."

"Wake up, Zoz, we must be on our way," Nicholas said, looking over to the lump where Zoz was sleeping. "Zoz, rise up!" There was no response. "Zoz, time to get up!" But Nicholas soon realized that Zoz was not there, just a blanket. "Zoz! Where are you?" he called. Getting up, Nicholas rushed outside to look for him, saying, "Oh he must have gone out to see his mountains in the daylight. Perhaps he has gone to gather firewood or berries. Zoz! Zoz! Where are you? Get back here." But there was no sign of him.

Rising, Sara said, "Yes, he must have gone to get a better look at the mountains and if he does not return soon, we will have to search for him." She felt confident that Zoz would return any minute. Stroking her horse, she said, "Storm, where did he go? You saw him, did you not? If only you could speak to me. I will start cooking breakfast and hopefully he will smell it and return to eat."

After Nicholas lit the fire, Sara cooked a bird. They ate, all the while keeping a watchful eye out for Zoz. Then as time passed, feeling quite concerned, Nicholas packed up their gear and was ready to leave but Zoz was still not back. He called out again, "Zoz! Zoz! Can you hear me?"

The princess yelled, "Zoz, Zoz. Are you hurt?"

Frustrated, Nicholas mounted Liberty and walked along the path for quite a distance to the left of the cave looking for him, but there was not a soul in sight. So then he trotted fairly far to the right of the cave. Still no sign of Zoz! The mountains, though beautiful, were massive. The peaks disappeared into the clouds. There was only one way to get to the land of Windsor and that would be over the mountain range. To go around would take far longer, time they did not have. With Old Bellow loose in the kingdom, there was no time to waste. Upon returning alone to the cave, Nicholas said, "The aroma of fresh roasted quail wafting through the air should have enticed any hungry soul, but Zoz did not show up." Feeling very uneasy, he added, "Sara, I fear that harm has come to our friend or else he has gone extremely far away. I have searched and searched the surrounding area to no avail, and we most certainly cannot put off our quest any longer. It is vital that we get to the wizard as soon as possible, so we must be on our way and hopefully meet up with Zoz, en route."

"It pains me but I have to agree with you, Nicholas. That is what we must do and I pray we will meet up with Zoz along the way," she responded.

So they set out without Zoz, to climb the mountain range to the other side, to the land of Windsor, guiding their horses very carefully along what seemed to be a deliberate narrow path leading upward toward the peak. While they progressed up, Nicholas noticed fewer trees than at the base of the mountain and the crystal rocks loosened underfoot from time to time. All the while, Nicholas and Sara watched for Zoz and continued to call out his name, but there was no sign of him. Although racked with guilt and feeling very sad for going on without Zoz, Nicholas knew it was the right choice because of the pressing task he had undertaken for the king.

The sun rose higher in the sky and they were making good time up the lofty mountain, stopping every so often to allow the horses to rest and take a drink. Looking down in the direction whence they had come, they could see over the Black Forest, and across the badlands to the plains. They tried to see their own hamlet of Ivan, but it was too far away. Remembering the kiss Princess Sara had blown to him when he left, distracted Nicholas. He wondered what was going to become of their friendship. Having her with him was a real comfort.

"Sara, we must move more swiftly to the land of Windsor and the wizard so that I can destroy Old Bellow and return home," he said in earnest

"You mean, *we* can destroy Old Bellow," said Sara, smiling at Nicholas.

Onward and upward they went, anxiously calling to Zoz every once in a while. As they neared the crest of the mountain, it grew much colder and they could see their breath. Since the air was thinner, the higher they got, they found it increasingly hard to take deep breaths. Sara felt a snowflake melt on her eyelid as snow started to float down from the sky. At first it was a gentle, pretty snowfall, but it soon got heavier, forcing them to pull up the hoods of their cloaks. When it got heavier still, Nicholas decided to put animal hides on the horses and get out their fur coats. The wind whipped up and it was getting icy underfoot, forcing them to guide Liberty and Storm very carefully, watching their footing. Now and then the chargers slipped. Nicholas and Sara's teeth chattered and the bitterly cold wind howled around them.

"Oh, Sara, are you well enough?" he asked her. "I know how cold you must be, but we have to keep going until we can find some shelter."

"I will be fine, Nicholas," she replied, not wanting him to know that she was very uncomfortable. An hour later, their fingers and toes were so cold that they feared they would lose them to frostbite and Nicholas secretly began to worry that they might not survive the storm, with no shelter in sight. Their eyebrows were stiff and white with ice and their ears ached except for the tips that were so numb they felt pointed. Princess Sara desperately held the reins, worried she might be blown off her horse. The wind raged fiercely and the snow slapped against her face, stinging and making the visibility extremely poor. It was a white-out. They could no longer see where they were going.

All of a sudden, Liberty slipped off the trail, hurling Nicholas from the saddle and over the side of the mountain. "SARAAAA!" he screamed in horror, plummeting downward. Reaching out, he caught hold of a tree branch on the mountainside with his numb hands, halting his fall. Grasping it as tightly as he could with both hands, Nicholas tried to pull himself back up onto the ledge, but the limited feeling in his fingers made it impossible and he let loose with his right hand and dangled there. "I cannot hold on any longer," he yelled as a great sense of doom washed over him. He lost his grip with his left hand and hurtled off the mountain again. "Ahhhhhhhh!" he cried as he fell down, down. Sara watched in horror, unable to do anything to help him. The thought of losing Nicholas was gut wrenching. But out of nowhere, the extraordinary white eagle swooped under him, catching him on its back. The giant bird whisked Nicholas back up and onto the mountain trail to safety beside Sara and, in the blink of an eye, it had disappeared once again.

Now, they knew that this eagle was very special but didn't know how or why it kept coming to the rescue. Extremely ruffled by this near disaster, Nicholas clutched Sara, who had jumped off her horse, and hugged her for comfort and warmth. Sara kissed him and said, "You are all right now. I am here and we shall stay together."

"Oh, Sara, I don't want anything bad to happen to you," he said, quivering. After several minutes, Nicholas felt more composed. He yelled, "Zoz, Zoz! Where are you!?" In a while the snow started to ease up, allowing them to see their way again, so they cautiously continued up the mountain. Hours passed. The wind gradually died down and the snow storm finally came to an end, allowing them to pick up the pace. It wasn't much longer before they reached the summit. Only able to take very shallow breaths and practically frozen stiff, the couple stood there, atop the Crystal Mountain, looking down to where they yet had to travel. Nicholas spotted another cave. "Sara! Shelter!" he exclaimed excitedly, pointing. It took another fifteen minutes or so to reach the cave and, after lighting a torch, Nicholas peered in, "Oh, this is plenty large enough for all of us." So inside they went and claimed a space to camp. "It is a good thing I collected an extra amount of kindling last night," he said with relief. "I will build a fire so that we can warm up and thaw out." After getting a fire started, he threw dry blankets on Storm and Liberty and then he and the princess lay down on fur pelts and wrapped themselves in them to get warm. Unable to stop shivering, he gently massaged Sara's hands and feet to warm them, and then Sara massaged his. It was very painful as their fingers and toes began to thaw. They throbbed at first and then tingled with pins and needles, but eventually the feeling returned. Since it was late afternoon, Nicholas said, "We will stay here for the night, Sara, and get an early start in the morning."

"Yes, fine. I feel much better now, thank you. Tomorrow will be a better day, you will see," she said.

Pulling himself to his feet, Nicholas took another look out over the side of the mountain range. "Sara, I can see a lake, I think, but the water is a very unusual mustard colour. Beyond that there is some sort of odd-looking region but it does not appear to be trees." Squinting his eyes to see better, he said, "My goodness, it looks like giant toadstools! Once we get closer we will see for certain. How very strange. That must be the land of Windsor! Good night, dear lady. Sweet dreams."

"Good night, Nicholas. I will see you in the morrow," replied the princess. They nestled in for the night, but as he lay there in the glow of the fire, sleep eluded Nicholas, as all he could think about was the fact that so many people depended on him. He stared up at the beads of moisture on the ceiling of the cave and watched them drip into the wee hours of the morning. Come daybreak, after dozing off for only a short while, Nicholas got up. It was a frosty morning and the mountain glistened as the sun rose and shone upon it. He stirred up the fire and prepared something to eat and though he hesitated to disturb the princess because she looked so beautiful sleeping peacefully, he woke her up. They ate and then began their descent down the mountain.

"Sara, be very careful as there is still snow covering the trail." But as the sun rose, it started to melt the ice and snow. Although thinking it was less and less likely that they would meet up with Zoz again, the young man yelled out, "Zoz! Zoz!" But there was no response. Nicholas was sad at the thought that Zoz was gone. "Look, Sara, there is another of those huge ravens flying overhead." Feeling anxious about it, he said, "I feel as though it has been following us ever since we began this journey." They continued all day, down, down the side of the mountain and the air warmed up the farther down they went. Finally, Nicholas said wearily, "We should stop to rest and allow me to search for more food." A very strong gust of wind howled past them.

"Oh my goodness, suddenly the sky is growing very dark over there. Look at those billowing black rain clouds. I fear a bad storm is approaching," said Sara. Thunder rumbled off in the distance. Sheets of lightning lit up the sky. The storm blew closer to them. Again it thundered, much louder this time, as the storm was upon them. There was a flash of lightning very close by and the wind picked up even stronger. The swollen clouds opened up and torrential rain poured down.

Nicholas said, "We must find shelter."

"Look, down there," Sara pointed. "An overhang of rock that is not too far." They swiftly headed toward it, mud splashing up as they cantered along the trail. A tree stood nearby it and Nicholas took out a large animal hide and the couple worked to secure it from the tree to the overhang with some heavy boulders, hoping it would block some of the wind and rain. It continued to pour and the wind blew so fiercely that the hide didn't hold. The wind nudged one of the boulders aside and the hide flapped every which way, allowing the rain to soak them. It was a wall of rain and they could barely see through it. Thunder and lightning cracked all around them, which spooked the horses. Very agitated, Liberty neighed repeatedly. "Calm down. You will be all right, Liberty. We are here with you," Sara said in a soft, soothing voice to comfort the trembling horse. "The storm will pass soon, my friend. Do not be afraid."

Holding blankets over himself, Nicholas threw animal hides on the chargers to keep them as warm and dry as possible, but it was useless. There were huge gusts of wind that whipped the rain into their faces so hard that it hurt. Sara groaned and nestled her face into Nicholas's chest. He said, "Wait, let me get my shield to protect us." And then they huddled together against the rock, drenched and shivering, their soaked clothes clinging to their bodies. "Arrgh! I wish we were back in Ivan in my warm, cozy cottage," he said, disheartened. There was a fork of lightning and then thunder, and another and another as Mother Nature's fury was upon them. What seemed like hours passed as the pair endured the pelting downpour. The lightning lit up the night sky. The booming thunder and lightning got so close that Nicholas was sure they would be hit.

Then suddenly there was a deafening crack of thunder and at the same time a bolt of lightning struck the tree right next to them, splitting it in half; it burst into flames. Storm, spooked, neighed and bucked with fright and Sara ran to him and grabbed him, guiding him away from the burning tree, calming him down with her gentle voice, "Do not worry, my dear. We are fine. This will not last much longer. Soon we will be dry and warm again. There, there. At least the fire is giving off heat for us, ha ha ha."

Eventually, the rumbles of thunder moved farther and farther away and the length of time between the lightning and thunder was longer. The rain started to let up and finally ended. The wind died down and soon all seemed right with the world again as the clouds blew away to reveal the bright moon glowing in the sky. Yawning, Nicholas said under his breath, "I am so tired. It has been a long, hard day." Sleep proved easier that night and although they were soaking wet, they both fell fast asleep from exhaustion in each other's arms.

CHAPTER 8

THE WIZARD

The next morning, Nicholas and Sara, their clothing dry, were startled awake by a loud shrieking in their ears. It was the huge white eagle again. Wiping the sleep from his eyes, Nicholas said, "I get the distinct impression this bird wants us to follow it, Sara." So together they quickly packed up their gear and set off down the mountain. The giant bird circled overhead as they worked their way down the side of the mountain until they reached the foothills and then continued on to the yellow lake. Examining the body of water, Nicholas said with astonishment, "Have you ever seen such strange-coloured water before?"

"My goodness, no!" replied Sara. Although their supply of drinking water needed to be replenished, they were suspicious of the condition of this lake water and walked past it. The eagle shrieked and led them into the mushroom forest.

Scanning the area, Nicholas said in disbelief, "What a mysterious place this is. Instead of trees, we are walking through a forest of mushrooms, the size of trees."

"How very strange. I have never seen anything like it," answered the princess. An eerie thick smokelike mist covered the ground, leaving Nicholas a little nervous. It was then that they saw the legendary Wizard of Windsor ahead of them. Nicholas stood frozen, his heart pounding in his chest. "Nicholas!" gasped Sara, grabbing his hand and squeezing it tightly.

The great white eagle flew ahead to the very mystical looking old man wearing a white, full-length hooded robe and perched on his right forearm. The man's face was cloaked, except for his glowing, amber coloured eyes and long white beard. Considering the bird's impressive size, the man seemed to hold it effortlessly. Sara trembled with fear. As perspiration trickled down his forehead, Nicholas found it hard to swallow, his throat very dry. They had no idea what to expect.

"Do not fear, young ones. Come, Nicholas and Sara." said the wizard in a soft, gentle, comforting voice. "You seek the knowledge of the wise. There is great danger for you, and only I, Edwin, have the power to help you." Nicholas was astounded that the wizard knew of his quest.

"How do you know who we are and what we have to do," he asked.

The wizard chortled merrily, "Ha ha ha, lad, I know all things concerning this part of the world. My powers make it possible for me to see and hear many things. I know of the last dragon, Old Bellow, on the loose once again. There is only one logical explanation. My brother, Edgar, a very evil wizard must be responsible. He has tried many times to destroy my realm, since he does not have control over it, and each time I have used my powers to ward him off. But do not worry, I will help you save your kingdom. Many years before you were born, I helped a great knight from your kingdom vanquish the beast, Old Bellow, with a magic sword. I did not allow him to kill the dragon, but the knight had to touch him with the tip of the sword, which put a spell on the beast, making him sleep eternally."

"Yes, you speak of Sir Nigel, I know the tale well," remarked Nicholas.

"My brother must have somehow broken the spell, so I will have to use more powerful magic this time. I am a wizard of good, not evil. I will not allow you to slay the dragon but you may render it harmless. You are very brave to have travelled through the Black Forest and over the Crystal Mountains. I am certain my brother has had his eye on you," said the wizard.

"Sir, was it you who sent that eagle to help me in the quicksand and on the mountain?" asked Nicholas curiously.

"Yes, lad, I did. I could not bear to see your brush with death. I had to intervene with magic. I need you to save your kingdom," the wizard replied. "It is with pleasure that I share my magic with you. You must turn Old Bellow mellow with the water from the lake of yellow."

"But your wizardry, sir, I cannot possibly hope to get the dragon here to Yellow Lake. I would surely die just trying. There must be another way, another magic sword or something?" said Nicholas.

"Young man, I am the old wise one. You must trust me. You simply have to fill this flask with water from Yellow Lake and splash it on the dragon or get him to drink it and he will become gentle and passive for all time. He will never breathe fire again or be a threat to your land," the wizard assured them. "Not even my brother could undo this spell. Yellow Lake is the source of my magical power. I have tried for 200 years to lure Edgar here to push him into it. Only then would he become good and never harm anyone again. That is my quest. You must rest now and take nourishment. Then, go forth and conquer Old Bellow. But beware of strangers. All is not as it seems."

Nicholas and Sara were each led into giant mushroom cottages that were furnished with carved toadstool chairs, toadstool tables and beds, very cozy with a warm fire crackling. After giving them some kind of stew to eat and some ale to drink, the wizard told them to sleep for a while and then took Liberty and Storm to a resting area, removed their saddles, and fed them, as well. Several hours later they awoke feeling refreshed and the wizard called to them. He invited them to follow him to a very large crystal rock, and said, "Gaze upon this crystal and you will see your kingdom." What they saw was so horrifying: cottages in flames and people screaming and running wildly. They saw the dragon trampling through a village and breathing fire everywhere. Plumes of thick smoke rose above smouldering cottages while trees burned and the ground was charred black. Not recognizing the villages, Sara hoped that theirs was still safe. This was very upsetting. Waving his hand over the crystal, the wizard said, "I will show you someone you long to see." And there in the crystal rock Princess Sara saw her uncle, King William. The expression on his face was that of fear and hopelessness.

Imagining harm coming to him, her eyes welled up with tears. "Are these events happening right now or in the future?" she asked the wizard.

"This is the present, lass. But there is still time to save your kingdom. You must make haste now though," the wizard replied. He escorted them to their well-rested horses and replenished saddlebags.

Mounting his horse, Nicholas said, "Thank you for your kindness and help. I will make you proud. I will find Old Bellow and end his destructive rampage," and turned to leave.

The princess waved goodbye and said, "Thank you, sir. It has truly been an honour meeting you."

The wizard's parting words were, "Farewell, young ones and peace be with you. When you pause, you will find Zoz." Then he motioned the white eagle ahead of Nicholas to guide them out of the mushroom forest and toward Yellow Lake.

"What did the wizard mean, when you pause, you will find Zoz? When and where?" Nicholas and Sara were thrilled at the thought of meeting up with Zoz again. Once out of the mushroom forest they came to Yellow Lake and Nicholas stopped and picked up a long branch to test the sandy shoreline before venturing toward the water. Having had the terrifying experience with the quicksand, he was taking no chances. Upon determining that it was solid ground underfoot, he went to the lakeside and filled the flask with the magic mustard-coloured water that was to tame the fire-breathing dragon. He also filled the waterskin from his belt as a reserve in case he needed it. After strapping them to his saddle, they followed the eagle toward the Crystal Mountains and suddenly it disappeared again. They knew their way from there.

CHAPTER 9

FINDING ZOZ

They galloped on for a while and arrived at the base of the mountains. Although dreading the treacherous journey ahead, Nicholas knew that time was of the essence. "I am not looking forward to the return trip, Sara. How about you?" he said.

She swallowed and said adamantly, "Nor am I, Nicholas, but I know we will successfully track down Old Bellow and find Zoz, I just know it. Together, we can do anything!"

As the farmer looked up at the mountain range he spotted what looked like a person in a long, dark robe way up near the top on one of the ridges. "Look, up there! Maybe it is Zoz!" he said hopefully. "Zoz!" he called out. Then the figure simply vanished right before his eyes. "How strange; I must be taking leave of my senses, Sara. Never mind. Just continue on," he said.

Sara said, "I, too, have seen what I thought was a person back in the Black Forest, but he vanished. I do not think there is anything wrong with you. Someone is playing tricks on us." The sky was clear with no signs of storms as they cantered farther up the slope, along the trail, at a steady, brisk pace for hours, the climb getting steeper, the higher they went. As it grew darker, Nicholas started to look for shelter for the night and eventually spotted a cave opening and they made their way over to it. Jumping down from Liberty, Nicholas lit a torch and went inside to see if the cave was large enough to house both of them plus the horses. It was enormous and very high with large crystal spikes hanging from the ceiling. The moonlight shining through the cave opening made them sparkle. It was truly beautiful. They could hear the magnified echo of water dripping in the back of the cavern where they noticed a glowing. Something felt quite different about this cave, putting Nicholas on edge. The familiar uncomfortable feeling that something or someone was watching them bothered him, but he was so tired that he just gathered some twigs and brush to start a fire to keep them warm for the night. Sara tended to and fed the animals and gave Nicholas some dried game from her saddlebag to eat; after their meal, they went right to sleep.

In the morning, they were jolted awake by the loud echoing thud of a rock falling in the back of the cave. "Who goes there? Is that you, Zoz?" Nicholas demanded. "Zoz?" He walked back to where the cave narrowed and the sound of dripping water grew louder. It wasn't until he turned a corner that Nicholas caught sight of Zoz, to his surprise, on the far side of a luminous turquoise pool of water. "Sara, it is Zoz!" he yelled enthusiastically. Quivering and cowering up against the wall on a narrow ledge, Zoz's clothes were shredded and bloody and he had claw marks down his chest and a very deep gash on his thigh. His face was as white as a ghost; his eyes wide open with shock. Zoz didn't speak, something had terrified him. Swimming over to him in the frigid water, Nicholas said excitedly, "Oh Zoz. You are alive! It is me, Nicholas. Remember me from the Black Forest? We escaped together. You are safe now. It is all right. Oh, how wonderful to have found you." Sara ran to the area and was smiling from ear to ear at the news of finding Zoz.

Although when she saw his grave-looking condition she was very concerned. She waited on the other side of the pool.

As if not recognizing him, Zoz stared blankly at Nicholas, and then with a sudden outburst of terror, clutched Nicholas's arm and begged, "Please, do not leave me. Do not let it get me; it is going to kill me." He was so frightened.

"What is going to kill you, Zoz? What did this to you? What happened, Zoz? Why did you disappear?" asked Nicholas.

In a weak voice Zoz said, "Oh, Nicholas, it is you! Lad, that night we camped in the cave, I awoke and went out in the moonlight to look around and was attacked by a monstrous white hairy creature. Standing three metres high, it had huge, powerful paws with long claws and big, sharp teeth. It grabbed me and carried me here, where I was certain it was going to kill me. But surprisingly there was a loud noise that distracted it and it left the cave and has not yet returned." Getting himself worked up, he continued, "I am petrified that it will come back to finish me off. Did you not see it? I was badly mauled in the struggle. We must get away from here before it returns."

"Of course we will leave just as soon as possible, but I must tend to your wounds first," said Nicholas reassuringly. "This wound on your leg is very bad. You have lost quite a lot of blood. Let me bind it up with this." He tore off a piece of his sleeve and tightly wrapped it around Zoz's leg. "We have not seen or heard any sign of such a creature. We made it to the land of Windsor and met the wizard and we are on our way back to find the dragon, Old Bellow. I think we should try to get you out of here now."

"But I do not swim," said Zoz.

"Hold onto me then," said Nicholas and he started to swim back across the pool while carrying Zoz, piggyback style. Then suddenly, without warning, they heard Liberty and Storm neighing and snorting frantically as a ferocious growl rumbled through the cave. Heavy footsteps were approaching, which violently shook the cave.

Shuddering, Zoz screamed, "Noooooo!" and fell limp. It was the terrifying white hairy monster Zoz had described and it had come back for him. In the middle of the pool, his eyes like saucers, Nicholas froze for a second wondering what he could do. Looking at Sara, he gestured to her to move to a nook where the cave jutted out which would hide her from the monster's view. In a split second, he decided to continue across the pool to the same nook. Shaking Zoz and lightly slapping his cheeks, Nicholas revived Zoz from his faint.

He whispered, "Zoz, come on, man, wake up. We must hide from the monster," and they reached Sara just in time, before the monster turned the corner. The floor of the cave trembled beneath them with each step the monster took. The water in the pool splashed to and fro, making waves and the crystal spikes shook overhead. When the monster entered the large pool cavern, looking toward where he had left Zoz, it couldn't see him. It growled loudly in anger, which echoed throughout the cave. Holding his breath, Nicholas placed his arm in front of Sara, pressing her up against the wall of the cave so she would not be seen. Cautiously, he peered around the corner, and saw the monster go toward the pool to search for Zoz with his back to them. Clutching Zoz and grabbing Sara's hand, Nicholas tried to slip by it, shoving Sara ahead. With the weight of Zoz on his back, he couldn't move very fast and the monster spun around, savagely thrashing its claws at them and roaring wildly. It was a deep, deafening roar that made the cave rumble and shake tremendously. Suddenly, crystal spikes and boulders began crashing down all around them. The chargers neighed and bolted out of the cave. "Run quickly for the exit, Sara, or we will be buried and crushed to death. It is a cave-in!" yelled Nicholas. The white monster lurched toward them, its jaws open, revealing its enormous sharp teeth. But alas, at that very moment, a large crystal spike shook and loosened from the ceiling and fell with such force that it pierced the monster's head. With a loud boom, it fell lifeless to the floor in front of them. Nicholas, with Zoz still on his back, ran around the monster toward the cave opening. Crystal rocks were falling everywhere around them. Ahead, Sara tripped on something and fell down.

Pushing on the floor to get up, to her horror, she saw that she had tripped over a human skeleton. "Ahhhhhhh!" she screamed and swiftly took off out of the cave like a shot.

Nicholas, on her heels, jumped over the skeleton, also screaming, "Ahhhhhhh!" The moment they cleared the entranceway, an enormous piece of crystal crashed to the ground and the cave completely collapsed with tons of rock piling up, metres high, blocking the cave entrance. Then there was silence. The cave-in was over. The trio coughed, choking on the thick dust that filled the air around them. "We have made it! Sara, are you all right? Zoz, how about you? What a catastrophe!" said Nicholas as he lowered Zoz down to the ground.

"Yes," Sara said, coughing.

"Yes, lad, I will live. I have you to thank again. If not for you, that beast would certainly have killed me or I would have been trapped in the cave. It seems you are my guardian angel," Zoz said, wearily. The dust settled. Liberty and Storm returned to them, saddlebags intact. Then Sara finished cleaning and bandaging Zoz's wounds. She had a pouch of balsam salve to put on them.

"Did you see that skeleton?" Nicholas asked.

"Yes, I did," replied Sara, shuddering.

"I wonder who that poor soul was?" mused Nicholas, thinking of the terrible close call they had just experienced. Then he closed his eyes and in his mind he saw Princess Sara blow him that kiss. He let out a heavy sigh. The thought of that magical moment made him feel better. He stared at her lovingly. "Let us have something to eat and drink. You must gain your strength back, Zoz." He checked to see that the flask of yellow water was safe; Nicholas found it still secured to his saddle. "Thank goodness for that!" he said and built a fire and roasted a bird. A while later, Nicholas asked, "Are you feeling up to travelling now, Zoz?"

"Yes, lad, I can manage. If we take it slow. I feel stronger now that I have eaten. I hope there are no more of those creatures to run into." Nicholas helped Zoz up onto Liberty, and the two of them started up the mountainside, Sara following behind, with thoughts of their run-in with the enormous white monster fresh in their minds. Every so often, the horses tripped and stumbled on loose rocks and pieces of crystal. Up, up, and still higher they rode all day as the sun rose in the sky. But as the air grew colder and their breath formed little clouds, they were forced to put coats on. Despite the obstacles they had encountered, thoughts of Old Bellow destroying their village spurred them on until they reached the summit where the air was thinner and they found it more difficult to breathe. It began to snow but it was a light snowfall. There were no high winds this time. They all looked down the other side of the mountain and could see the Black Forest off in the distance. Looking at each other, each knew what the other was feeling: reluctance to head down toward that evil.

"Well, I think it is time to rest for the night anyway. I will erect a shelter with animal hides and tree branches," said Nicholas. "Zoz, you are still weak and exhausted, you should just lie down and go to sleep. I will keep watch." In his mind, Nicholas kept seeing the skeleton they had seen in the cave. His thoughts kept drifting to the monster that had taken Zoz. *What if there are more of them?* But he kept it to himself so as not to upset the others. Feeling ruffled, he kept one hand on the handle of his sword. Sitting there on watch for the night, he listened to the distant howling of wolves and wondered if he and the others would also end up being skeletons discovered by someone one day. He made sure he didn't fall asleep and kept the fire lit all night to ward off any wild beasts.

Before sunrise Nicholas roused Sara and Zoz. "My friends, it is time to get up and get ready to head down the mountain. All we have to do is survive that, get through the dreaded Black Forest, and track down Old Bellow. We can do it. We have endured so much already." The weather was fair as they ate but no one was very talkative. Nicholas saddled up the horses and they hit the trail. The trip seemed easier this time. The ice had melted and there was just a thin blanket of snow on the path. They stopped at regular intervals to rest, eat, and drink and by late afternoon they were nearing the base of the mountain. It was only then that the sky began to darken with large, grey, ominous-looking rain clouds overhead.

Rubbing his chin while giving thought to the situation, Nicholas said, "We should probably set up camp now because it looks as though a storm is brewing. Then in the morrow we will be approaching the forbidden forest rested and alert. What do you think?"

Zoz said, "Yes, lad, I agree. Let me help you erect a shelter quickly before the rain starts."

Princess Sara said, "No, Zoz, do not be ridiculous. You need to rest your wounds. I will help Nicholas and quickly gather some kindling and get some food ready for us."

Then as if someone suddenly unzipped the clouds, the rain began to pour down. Sara and Nicholas scrambled to set up a lean-to with animal hides and branches and got a fire going. Then the travellers sat around it and ate, exchanged stories, and chuckled as it teemed straight down around them. There was no wind to speak of so they managed to stay fairly dry under the shelter. Although very tired from lack of sleep, Nicholas listened keenly to Zoz, who was a very witty man and had led an extremely interesting life as a troubadour who sang and acted in pageants on wagons that travelled from place to place. They had become very close friends in spite of their age difference. Sara, who had never kept company with common people before this, was so impressed by their intellect and genuine kindness. She was really enjoying herself.

Then, changing the mood, Nicholas asked seriously, "Zoz, if we manage to get through the forest alive, do you want us to take you home to your shire or would you like to join us on our pursuit of Old Bellow? I warn you though, it will be very risky."

Zoz answered, "Lad, I would be honoured to stay with you and Sara as long as you feel I would not stand in the way of your success. I have no family now to return to."

"Good, it is settled then," Nicholas said happily. The heavy downpour was short-lived but it continued to lightly drizzle through the night. This night, against Nicholas's wishes, Sara insisted that she keep watch while Nicholas got some much-needed sleep, feeling that Zoz wasn't up to the task. Sitting by the fire watching in all directions for any dangers, the princess felt so content to be sharing this time with Nicholas. This must be what love feels like, she thought. She couldn't wait to find Old Bellow, take care of him, and spend the rest of her life with her hero. She knew her uncle would approve. By morning the sky had cleared and the sun was shining brightly and the mountain glistened. Nicholas awoke, cleared his throat and said, "Zoz, Sara, I dreamt of a plan for when we reach the forest. Now that we know what to expect in there, I think we must be very watchful and gallop straight through as fast as possible without stopping to rest. If we hack the foliage with our swords along the way, as long as we do not hesitate or stop, hopefully, the bats, snakes, and mole people will not get a chance to attack us. What do you think?"

"I agree with you. That seems like a good plan, our only hope," said Sara, convinced it would work.

Zoz asked, "Why do we have to go through the forest at all? Can we not just go around it?"

"Oh, no, Zoz, that would take days longer and you know we just do not have that much time. There is no telling what devastation Old Bellow could have done by the time we got back to Ivanshire. Our village could be reduced to ash by then." They prepared their chargers and began their final descent, almost blinded by the dazzling sunlight reflecting on the crystal, watching for any dangerous monsters along the way. A large raven squawked and circled overhead, and then Nicholas saw the familiar dark figure of a man at the base of the mountain in the distance. Wiping the hair from his eyes, he said, "Sara and Zoz, do you see that person down there?"

"Yes," they both said,

"Where did he come from and I wonder who he is?" said Zoz.

Nicholas said, "I have seen him a few times over the course of my journey and he always seems to mysteriously vanish before I can get to him. It is very disturbing." With caution, they headed to the spot where the person stood and the next thing they knew, he melted into a black puddle before their very eyes.

"Oh my goodness," said Zoz, looking at the puddle.

"What is going on?" said Sara.

"You see what I mean? This is not natural, it must be magic. I thought I was going mad, but now you are witnesses to it, as well."

"This must have something to do with the wizard Edgar, the evil brother of the Wizard of Windsor," said Sara. "He warned us that we could encounter him. We must make haste and get through the forest right away."

CHAPTER 10

THE EVIL BROTHER

They approached the Black Forest and recognized the two trees with the cut marks that they had previously squeezed between. Entering the dim forest, Nicholas whispered, "We will have to stay here and wait until our eyes get used to the darkness." They heard the creaking noises as the vines and branches entwined and closed up the opening again, making them prisoners. Sara cringed and took a deep breath and focused on their plan to ride nonstop until they reached the other side.

"Whatever you think, Nicholas, I am just along for the ride and cannot see a thing at the moment," said Zoz. He wrapped his arms around Nicholas's waist. Trembling in the silence, they waited until the trees started to come into focus.

"Can you see now, Sara?"

"Yes, somewhat, Nicholas. My eyes have adjusted. We should go. Lead on."

"OK, then, hold on for your life, Zoz." Zoz clenched tighter around Nicholas's waist and they swiftly galloped along the path, guided only by the very faint glow of light they could see filtering through the trees from the opposite side of the woods. Holding the reins tightly with one hand, Nicholas vigorously slashed his sharp sword nonstop through hanging vines, clearing the way, with his other. Storm followed directly behind Liberty. Sara also swung her sword from side to side to protect herself, not taking her eyes off Nicholas and Zoz. *Cloppity, cloppity, cloppity* was the only sound to be heard. They didn't encounter any mole creatures or snakes or any other threats as they flew through the forbidden forest. Liberty, puffing and panting, stayed to the path and ducked from obstructions, when unexpectedly, a huge swarm of bees exploded up from the side of the trail, surrounding them. All they could hear was a thunderous buzzzzzzzzzzzzzzz. . . . There were hundreds of them, maybe thousands, swirling around their heads and landing on them, stinging them. "Ahhhhhh, ouch, ouch!" the trio cried out as they were repeatedly stung. Each sting felt like a burn on their skin. The horses, too, were stung multiple times and neighed frantically and veered from the path to evade them. Picking up the pace, the bees trailed behind them. Liberty and Storm dashed on rapidly and eventually they outran the swarm.

"Phew!" said Nicholas. "That was horrible. Are you well, Sara and Zoz?"

"Yes, lad, I am very sore with many stings, but I will be fine."

"I am stung as well but we must keep going before any creatures come," Sara said in a panic.

"You are right. Hyah, Liberty, hyah!" he said and again they galloped off in the direction of the light. At the same time, Nicholas heard a loud rustling sound behind them and swung his head back to look. Horrified, he saw a group of the mole creatures running after them, aiming spears at Sara, who was in the rear. They were sprinting extremely fast, so Nicholas yelled to her to hasten and she dug her heels into Storm a couple of times. Zoz gripped tighter around Nicholas's waist as Liberty sped up and the mole creatures threw their spears at them and missed. Suddenly, a mole creature jumped down from a tree onto Nicholas's shoulders, between him and Zoz, and grasped hold of his neck. Terrified, Zoz pounded its head repeatedly with his fist and pushed the mole creature as hard as he possibly could. It flew off and onto the ground as Liberty and Storm whizzed past and well beyond. Finally the furry creatures quit their pursuit and retreated and the three riders didn't stop until they found themselves at the other side of the forest. They frantically searched for an opening in the outer wall of trees but couldn't see one. Jumping down from his horse, Nicholas started hacking into a tree trunk and cutting vigorously with his sword but the branches and vines magically tangled and closed up the opening again. Soldiering on, he said, "Zoz, help to pull the vines apart while I cut." Sara jumped down and helped, thrusting her blade into the tangle. Persisting to slash faster and harder, they successfully made an opening large enough for Sara to squeeze through and then Zoz and Nicholas. But then they had to enlarge the opening for the horses to fit through.

Zoz and Sara held a tangle of vines on either side of the opening with all their might. The old man encouraged him saying, "Hurry, lad, you can do it. It is almost large enough." Seeing the trees move tighter together, Nicholas kept whittling away at it until his determination paid off and there was an opening large enough for the steeds to fit through. He quickly led them and they exited the Black Forest before the opening closed.

"Hurrah!" they cheered simultaneously.

Gasping, Nicholas looked at the swollen red welts from the bee stings all over himself and the others and said, "Oh my Lord, look at us." Sara hastened to gather mud to spread on them to cool the burning sensation. Nicholas checked their supplies and was pleased to find everything in place. After a while, feeling soothed, they agreed to proceed to the arid badlands and search for Old Bellow to confront him once and for all.

It was hot and dry in the badlands region and after several hours, Nicholas insisted on stopping. "We must stop and rest for a while and have a drink before continuing on. Fortunately, the sun will soon be setting so it will cool down and be more comfortable. We are getting low on our water supply though and we will have to drink sparingly until we can replenish at the river on the plains."

Shrugging his shoulders, Zoz said, "We will be fine, lad. Do not worry. I can go for very long stretches without water. When I travelled and performed with the minstrel guild we often went without water for long periods"

The princess said, "Do not worry about me. I am fine." After rationing some leftover dried cooked game that she had in her pouch, Sara fed Liberty and Storm some oats. They all sipped a small quantity of water and then, feeling refreshed, they set off, spewing a trail of dust in their wake, as a waning moon rose in the sky and shone on the hard, barren ground, dimly lighting their way.

Not wanting to lose any time, Nicholas said, "I just want to complete the mission and get home, so let us keep going and not sleep yet." But the young man didn't know where to expect Old Bellow at this point in time, so they headed in the familiar direction toward the plains. Galloping a while longer, they finally reached the plains and began making their way to the river.

Suddenly, Zoz said, "What is this? This is impossible!" What they saw was very baffling. What had just been grassy plains was now a sandy desert, complete with dunes, cacti, and lizards. The moon in the night sky turned into a blazing sun in daytime. The region had changed in the blink of an eye from night to day.

"What on earth is going on here? That was the plains! It should be the grassy plains! I do not understand what is happening. Some sorcery is at work here," Nicholas exclaimed. Now they were surrounded by desert, under a searing hot sun, and had no choice but to keep going. The punishing heat forced the guys to strip off their tunics to get relief. Even Sara had to strip down to her underclothes. Sweating profusely, they continued on. Gesturing ahead, Nicholas said, "Look there, in the distance. Do you see the dark grey smoke? That must be the result of Old Bellow's wrath. He must be close. We must hasten and stop him."

They were getting weaker and weaker from the sweltering heat, their skin was sunburned and blistering. It was taking a heavy toll on them so they drank some more water only to realize that they were nearly out. The horses weren't able to keep up a very good pace through the shifting sandy terrain that seemed to go on forever and they slowed from a trot to a painfully slow walk while Zoz hunched over onto Nicholas. Wondering if they would survive this dreadful situation, Nicholas slid down from the saddle to lighten the load for Liberty's sake. From the corner of his eye he noticed two lizards scurry behind a spiny cactus and several large black crows circled overhead. Suddenly there was a cold rush of air and a dark shadow appeared in the distance ahead of them. It wavered from side to side.

"There is that person again!" cried Sara. Then the figure instantly floated over the sand toward them, as if on wheels and stood before them. It was a mysterious looking man with a long silver beard, wearing a full-length, black hooded robe. Perched on his arm was a huge black raven.

With his hood up, the man's face was not visible except for his eyes, which glowed fiery red. He spoke in a raspy voice. "So the heroes have arrived at my detour! Surely you do not think that I can allow you to continue on and harm my dragon. No! No, you will not reach your destination, but instead you will bake in this desert and die of thirst. Hahaha."

Barely able to speak, Zoz lowered himself from the horse and whispered in a thin voice, "Who is this, Nicholas? Are you acquainted with this evil soul?"

"You must be Edgar, the brother of the Wizard of Windsor," Sara said in dismay. "Why are you here interfering with our task? How could you allow Old Bellow to destroy villages and ruin people's lives? How could you be so evil when your brother is so good? Please, you must turn the desert back into the plains and let us be on our way."

But the wicked conjurer just laughed. "Ha ha ha ha ha, you make me laugh, my young, naive princess. I use my powers to get what I want, not to rescue little mortals like you. You mortals are an abomination that I would sooner eradicate. As far as your eyes can see will be my domain when I am finished. I will rule here. Old Bellow is my trusted companion who will clear the way for me. Then Edwin will see that I am more powerful than him."

Just then, Liberty collapsed in the sand from heat exhaustion and Zoz started to gag and cough uncontrollably. "Water, water!" he begged.

There were only a few drops of water left and Nicholas, being the kind soul that he was, said, "Of course Zoz, it is yours, I will get it for you." Looking equally weak, he pleaded one last time with Edgar, "Please, return the plains back to normal and let us be."

"I am afraid not, my young lad," chuckled the evil wizard as he snatched the flask from Nicholas's saddle, intending to drink the water before Zoz had a chance to quench his thirst. Little did he know that it was not regular drinking water in that flask but the yellow water from Yellow Lake. The wicked Edgar poured it down his throat and cried out, "Ahhhhhhhhh! What have you done?" They looked on in astonishment as Edgar fell to his knees and writhed about. Then his glowing red eyes turned amber like his brother's. In a few minutes, the expression on his face softened and he said, "Ohhh, I am so very, very sorry for what I have done. I have been so terribly bad. Please find it in your hearts to forgive me. I will make it up to you."

Sternly, Nicholas said to him, "As long as you realize that good, not evil, is the way to be and that good must rule, you will be powerful. Your brother knows that and I am sure that he will be delighted to learn that you have changed. You should reunite with him and allow us to deal with Old Bellow."

Edgar begged, "Oh, please do not harm Old Bellow. He is the last of his kind and is a truly remarkable creature. I could never forgive myself if anything bad happened to him."

"Do not worry, I will not harm him. He will only be subdued, I promise," Nicholas said in earnest. So Edgar turned the desert back into the grassy plains for them, with the river beside them and a bushy clump of trees for some needed shade. Taking his leave in the direction of the forbidden forest, Edgar vanished from their sight.

CHAPTER 11

OLD BELLOW

Immediately, Nicholas and Sara helped Zoz over to the river, where they immersed themselves and felt instant relief. Nicholas coaxed Liberty and Storm in, as well. They splashed about with a sense of victory knowing that the wizard, Edgar, would no longer do anyone harm. The horses whinnied with pleasure. They drank the water, which felt so good going down their parched throats, and then they rested under the shade trees until they felt rejuvenated. Then changing into dry clothes, Sara and Nicholas finally put on their armour and helmets, and grabbed their shields, in anticipation of meeting up with Old Bellow. Now was the time to muster all their courage and they galloped toward the billowing smoke. It was darker and thicker now and as they continued on, all they could smell was smoke. Sara and Nicholas were worried about what they would discover when they reached their own village and Nicholas was thinking about not letting anyone down.

"We must hasten, for I fear our village will be in ruins by the time we arrive," he urged Sara. Giving Liberty a slap on the rump, he said, "Faster, Liberty, faster, boy." Eventually he said, excitedly, "Zoz, this is it. We are home at last!" At first, all they could see was a wide swath of the charred frames of cottages and barns and as they neared the inner village, a couple of cottages and shops had burned to the ground and were smouldering.

"Oh, Lord," said Sara. "This looks grim. I pray Uncie is all right." The blacksmith's stable was in flames and the wool shop was smouldering.

"ROOOAR!" they heard from a distance away. The ground vibrated beneath them. Swallowing, Nicholas surveyed the area and then from the corner of his eye, he spotted the beast in the village square. There it stood, the colossal last dragon, towering above the highest trees, with enormous wings, moss green in colour.

Bug eyed, Nicholas pulled on the reins to stop Liberty. "Whoa, Liberty." He was unable to move. Nothing he had ever experienced in his life had prepared him for this.

"Old Bellow!" Sara exclaimed. She looked at Nicholas with alarm.

"ROOOAR!" the dragon bellowed again, a loud deep roar and flames of fire spewed out of its gigantic mouth in the direction of a thicket of trees, igniting it. There were no people to be seen.

Nicholas assumed they had all fled for their lives. Looking back at Zoz, he said, "You must go now with Sara, my friend, to the castle for safety. This is not your battle. I will meet up with you both when this is over."

With fear in his eyes, Zoz looked at Nicholas and apprehensively jumped down off Liberty's back and said, "Good luck, lad. I will be praying for you."

Sara said, "No, Nicholas, I want to stay and help you. I am not leaving."

But this time Nicholas put his foot down and insisted, "Your Highness! I am so thankful to have had your company and help on this journey. You have faced more than your fair share of dangers, but I will not allow you to remain here now. This is my duty. Please listen to reason and take Zoz to safety in the castle. I beg you! I promise I will see you later."

The princess responded, "Oh, Nicholas, my brave, brave hero. Be very careful. You must succeed or I shall die without you." She walked Storm directly beside Liberty and hugged and kissed Nicholas until he pried her off. Zoz got onto Storm behind the princess and they rode off in the direction of the hill where the castle stood. Nicholas hoped there would be guardsmen and soldiers there to protect them. Meanwhile, sitting tall in the saddle in his shining armour, he took a deep breath and approached the deserted town square. With a tremendous thud, Old Bellow turned and caught sight of Nicholas. Glaring at him with his red eyes, he slammed his monstrous tail down on the ground in anger and bellowed once more. "ROOOAR!" The ground shook violently. Old Bellow's nostrils flared, releasing smoke into the air.

Holding the reins tightly, Nicholas said to Liberty, "Steady, boy, steady." His heart was pounding and his eyes stung as sweat trickled down from his brow. *This is it. He is going to breathe fire on us now*, he thought to himself.

A panicky feeling came over him, but he mustered all his courage. Drawing his sword from its sheath, Nicholas grabbed his shield. Then in his mind he heard the Wizard of Windsor say, "You must turn Old Bellow mellow with the water from the lake of yellow." Knowing he had to act fast in order to save the village, he rode up as close as he could to the dragon, which came at him and let out another deafening roar. Old Bellow thrust his head from side to side. Nicholas retreated. The beast advanced toward the brave farmer and breathed fire at him, just missing him. A patch of grass directly in front of him burst into flames, scorching his clothes and singeing his hair. Feeling the heat, Nicholas began to hyperventilate.

Liberty neighed and bucked. Hiding his own fear, Nicholas held the reigns tightly and assured him, saying, "It is all right, Liberty. Steady. We can do this." The beast lurched his long neck from one side to another, thumping the ground in anger with his tail. The hero decided that his strategy would be to sneak behind the dragon when its head was farthest away from him. So when Old Bellow's head turned, the young man quickly circled around and galloped behind the dragon. When he was out of Old Bellow's visual range, Nicholas jumped down from his horse, tossed his shield aside, and grabbed the flask. Liberty sniffed at Nicholas, who slapped his rear end, forcing him to run away. Then just as he was preparing to leap up onto the dragon's tail, Old Bellow turned toward him. It could have been the end of Nicholas, but from out of nowhere, Sara, on Storm, appeared on the other side of Old Bellow. Clutching her sword with both hands, she stabbed his front leg to distract him, which worked. With his attention now on the princess, the dragon turned his back on Nicholas, allowing him to jump up onto his tail and climb higher onto his back. Old Bellow breathed out a stream of fire toward Sara, barely missing her as she bolted out of the way. Then feeling Nicholas on his back, he tried to throw him off by thrashing his tail to and fro. The young man grabbed hold of one of his wings and held on with all his might, the flask nestled under his right arm. The dragon tried to shake Nicholas off by flailing back and forth, roaring loudly. "ROOOAR." The earth trembled beneath them. The beast leapt up high into the air and took flight across the town square, dipping and tipping to force Nicholas off. Very alarmed, our hero was forced to release his sword and struggled to hold onto the flask as well as the dragon, so as not to fall off.

As Old Bellow flew more erratically, Nicholas opened the flask. He found he couldn't hold on any longer and dropped it onto the hard, leathery surface of the dragon's tail. The magical yellow water spilled out onto Old Bellow, who let out a thunderous roar and attempted to spew fire, only to find nothing come out. The bellows ceased and suddenly the beast landed and kneeled down with a thud, allowing Nicholas to jump off. Old Bellow, the last dragon, hung his head and moaned and groaned for a few minutes. He had no more fire.

Catching his breath, Nicholas was confident that the wizard's magic had taken effect and that Old Bellow was now mellow. Sara rode up and joined him. They approached the dragon's face and looked into his enormous eyes that had turned amber in colour. Sara stroked his cheek, saying, "Good boy. Now go to the plains and never return here. There is plenty of room there for you to roam and live out your days without disturbing anyone and enough vegetation there and in the Black Forest for you to eat for a lifetime." As if understanding what she said, the dragon stood up, looked at her and Nicholas with sorrowful eyes, and departed in the direction of the plains. The ground shook with each step. Eventually, he could no longer be seen and the vibrations stopped.

CHAPTER 12

SIR NICHOLAS

A ssuming that Old Bellow was far enough away to never bother them again, Nicholas was satisfied and retrieved his silver sword and shield from the ground. He hugged Sara and she kissed him and said, "Thank you for saving the kingdom."

Nicholas said, "Thank you for saving me!" Minutes later, Zoz ran over to them and the other villagers slowly began to return and gather in the village square, applauding and yelling in unison, "Hurrah, Nicholas!" Nicholas whistled for Liberty, who cantered over.

"Bravo, lad. You have saved us. Are you harmed?" asked Zoz.

"No, Zoz. I will be fine now. I am very happy it is over," he said with a deep sigh. "I could not have done it without Sara." Looking around the village, he observed, to his delight, that the damage wasn't as widespread as he had feared. The majority of the buildings were still intact and there was already a brigade of villagers frantically fetching pails of water from the river to douse the fires that still burned.

King William rode up to them on horseback. "Your Grace!" exclaimed Nicholas. Princess Sara smiled at her uncle, who climbed down from his charger.

He approached them, saying, "I am so happy that you are safe." He hugged Sara and said, "Young lady, you are a sight! I was so worried about you. It is a miracle that you are all right. You need to see the physician immediately and we will talk later." Then putting his arm around Nicholas's shoulder, he said, "I am very proud of you, lad! You have done a magnificent thing, successfully vanquishing the evil threat against my kingdom and you will be rewarded for this courageous victory. You have my everlasting gratitude. There will be a grand celebration and ceremony tomorrow after you have cleaned up, eaten, and had a good night's sleep. You and your friend are invited to spend the night in the castle as our honoured guests. I will have my personal physician take care of you both. Princess Sara will escort you. Oh and I thank you for taking care of her for me." The princess took Nicholas's hand and they set off toward the castle with Zoz.

"I am so very proud of you, Nicholas. I was afraid that Old Bellow would kill you and that you would not be in my life, but he did not and you have saved us all."

When they reached the castle, she showed Nicholas and Zoz to their bed chambers where they were immediately attended to by the royal physician and fed like princes and then they both fell fast asleep as soon as they lay down on the extremely comfortable feather-stuffed beds. Liberty and Storm were taken to the royal stables and fed and groomed. The princess was also treated by the royal physician and she bathed, ate, and went to sleep. King William planned a lavish feast and ceremony and when Nicholas and Zoz finally awoke the next day, they were provided with a fresh suit of clothes and guided to the dining hall. They were greeted with great fanfare when they entered. Horns played and a crowd of noble lords and ladies cheered for joy. Even Nicholas's friends were there to honour him. He was to be knighted for his bravery and valour. Princess Sara, dressed in a beautiful purple velvet gown, joined Nicholas and whispered something in his ear. They both giggled and looked at each other lovingly and sat beside each other at the head table. Zoz sat on the other side of Nicholas.

King William stood up and said to Nicholas, "Nicholas O'Hara, come hither. Now please kneel down before me." Then with his sword, he proceeded to tap Nicholas on each shoulder two times, saying, "By the power vested in me, I, William, king of Everland, do hereby dub thee Sir Nicholas, for saving this kingdom and for your acts of bravery. Now rise up, gallant knight." The guests cheered joyfully, the horns played, and food and drink were served. Everyone celebrated. There was music and dancing. Nicholas had never felt so loved and happy in his life.

Later, King William took Nicholas aside and said, "Sir Nicholas, Sara tells me that she loves you and I sense you return those feelings. What are your intentions for her?"

"Your grace, I do love her and intend to ask for her hand in marriage. Would you give us your blessing?" replied Nicholas.

The king smiled and said, "I would be honoured and proud to have you in the family," and motioned Sara over to them, leaving them alone together.

Nicholas took Sara's hands and kneeled in front of her on one knee, saying, "I love you, my dear lady, and would like nothing more than to spend the rest of my life with you. Could you find it in your heart to be my wife?"

The princess replied, "Oh, yes, Nicholas. I have thought of nothing else since we met. I would be proud to be your wife." The couple embraced and kissed.

To the delight of the kingdom, Sir Nicholas and Princess Sara had a lavish wedding and in the years to come they would have three children and pass on the legendary stories of the heroic adventures of Sara, Nicholas, and the last dragon. Zoz took over

Nicholas's farm and they remained dear friends. Old Bellow lived out his days as a gentle creature chomping on the grass of the plains and the vines and leaves of the trees in the Black Forest, which magically turned brighter, greener, and less daunting after that. In fact, the mole creatures loved the company of the dragon as it gave them rides every day for hours. As far as anyone knew, the Wizard of Windsor and his brother were happily reunited and living peacefully in the Mushroom Forest.

Sara felt something tickle her nose, causing her to open her eyes. A leaf had fallen from the tree above her and landed on her face. She had dozed off. "Oh, my, what time is it?" she said out loud. "Mother will be home soon." Looking up, she noticed that the clouds had blown away and the sun was high in the sky. The man in the crane working on the power lines was gone. She guessed it was lunch time, but for some reason she didn't feel very hungry. Instead, she thought she would rather get dressed and walk down to the mailbox at the corner to post the letter she had written to her Uncle William earlier. As she passed by Nicholas's house, from the corner of her eye, Sara spotted someone walking up the path to the front door. Feeling empowered and braver than usual, she turned her head to look and saw that it was Nicholas.

Seeing her, he smiled and said, "Hello," as he went into the house. Sara's heart skipped a beat. Suddenly, she had a reason to look forward to the new school year.

THE END